ALIEN ENCOUNTERS
IN ANGEL GROVE

To my mother,
who taught me not to fear the monsters,
but to embrace them
—GPC

PENGUIN YOUNG READERS LICENSES
An Imprint of Penguin Random House LLC

™ and © 2018 SCG Power Rangers LLC. Power Rangers and all related logos, characters, names, and distinctive likenesses thereof are the exclusive property of SCG Power Rangers LLC. All Rights Reserved. Used Under Authorization. Published by Penguin Young Readers Licenses, an imprint of Penguin Random House LLC, 345 Hudson Street, New York, New York 10014. Manufactured in China.

Photo credits: (used throughout):
half moon and starry space: RomoloTavani/iStock/Thinkstock,
Polaroid frame: eurobanks/iStock/Thinkstock,
purple nebula and cosmic dust: ClaudioVentrella/iStock/Thinkstock.

Designed by Gabriel P. Cooper with Olivia Kane

ISBN 9781524787264 (pbk)   10 9 8 7 6 5 4 3 2 1
ISBN 9781524788612 (hc)   10 9 8 7 6 5 4 3 2 1

MIGHTY MORPHIN
POWER RANGERS
™

ALIEN ENCOUNTERS
IN ANGEL GROVE

DOCUMENTED BY
GABRIEL P. COOPER

PENGUIN YOUNG READERS LICENSES
AN IMPRINT OF PENGUIN RANDOM HOUSE

A WORD FROM BULK AND SKULL

FARKAS BULKMEIER AND EUGENE SKULLOVITCH HAVE HAD THE UNFORTUNATE EXPERIENCE OF BEING PRESENT DURING MORE ALIEN ENCOUNTERS THAN ANYONE OTHER THAN THE POWER RANGERS.

How they found themselves in this situation remains unknown. Over the years, they've become Angel Grove's go-to eyewitnesses in the pursuit of truth. I was lucky enough to receive a call from both "Bulk" and "Skull" regarding their experiences and, with their permission, have reproduced a portion of their responses below.

"I have always said that if the Power Rangers hadn't been around, I could've handled the situation. Others will say, 'How would that even be possible? You don't have superpowers! You couldn't possibly fight monsters like the Power Rangers do!' Those people are wrong. But I guess we'll never know because the Power Rangers were always there, sucking up all the glory. Yeah . . . I could've done it. I've been face-to-face with these monsters! I even saved them once from that silly mirror monster! If it hadn't been for me, the Power Rangers would've been squashed a long time ago."

—FARKAS "BULK" BULKMEIER

"We saw a lot of monsters. Yeah, lots and lots of monsters. And if Bulk tells you that we know who the Power Rangers are, he's lying. We pretended to be the Power Rangers once. Thought it'd woo some ladies. Then we got attacked by a monster so . . . that didn't work. Thankfully the real Power Rangers stopped that monster. They always do. We're lucky to have them . . . don't tell Bulk I said that!"

—EUGENE "SKULL" SKULLOVITCH

CLASSIFICATION GUIDE

Throughout this book you will find a simple symbolic system at the top of each page for every being detailed. Below is a brief look at the symbols which will appear.

TYPE

Humanoid: These invaders closely resemble human beings in form.

Mythological: Drawn from our own stories, these invaders resemble familiar beings from legend.

Inorganic: Far more akin to something you'd find in your purse, pocket, or tool box than anything else.

Mammal: Covered in fur and having fangs, these aliens are similar to our earthbound furry friends.

Magic: Beings either born of magic or brought to our world with dominant mystical abilities.

Tech: More machine than flesh and blood, these monsters are wired up and overflowing with energy.

Insect/Arachnid: With either six legs or eight legs, they're equally creepy and definitely invasive.

Aquatic: Fish, frogs, and other freaks more frequently found beneath the waves or in shallow ponds.

Plant: These invaders' roots are no longer planted and are more likely to take oxygen away than give it.

Avian: Feathered beings with wings and razor-sharp beaks. Don't feed them. They'll keep coming back.

Reptilian: Scaly, scary, and with more teeth than necessary. You'll recognize them by their smile.

Unknown: Occasionally the Masters of the Moon whip up beings beyond recognition. Be not alarmed.

ORIGIN

EARTH   OUTER SPACE   MOON   UNKNOWN

TO HERE FROM WHERE? AND HOW?

SATELLITE IMAGE OF A CLASSIFIED MISSION TO THE MOON

FOR THOUSANDS OF YEARS THE PEOPLE OF EARTH ASSUMED THEY WERE ALONE IN THE UNIVERSE. WHEN THEY LOOKED UP AT THE NIGHT SKY AND SAW THE STARS, THEY ASSUMED THAT THEY WERE SPECIAL: THEY CONSIDERED THEMSELVES THE CENTER OF THE UNIVERSE.

As technology advanced, so, too, did our curiosity. We discovered that perhaps there was a chance we were wrong. At first, we looked at our own solar system and found our neighbors: Mercury, Venus, Mars, Jupiter, Saturn, Uranus, Neptune, and (at one point) Pluto. After that we peered farther and discovered our Milky Way galaxy. And beyond that? Beyond that we discovered an entire universe of galaxies, some similar to our own and some vastly different.

Suddenly the phrase *"we are alone in the universe"* became a question: Are we alone in the universe?

The attack on what would become Angel Grove by giant, humanoid rat creatures in the late eighteenth century; the mysterious crash landing of an unidentified flying object in Roswell, New Mexico, in 1947; and the escalated appearances of creatures such as the Mothman in Point Pleasant, West Virginia, in 1966 raised suspicions of alien visitors. While some would claim that the rat-monsters were costumes, the UFO was a fallen weather balloon, and the Mothman was simply a trick of lights, others were certain that the mystery of our place in the universe had begun to unravel.

And unravel it did.

The unexplained phenomena in Angel Grove, California, a miniature metropolis comfortably lying between mountains and the ocean, would forever change our world. While downtown Angel Grove featured modern architecture and bustling urban life, the residents of this fair city knew one another in a way more commonly found in small country towns. Whether you're grabbing one of Ernie's fresh and flavorful smoothies at the Angel Grove Youth Center, setting up a picnic at one of Angel Grove's lush parks, or throwing a volleyball back and forth on the beach, you're sure to meet more than one smiling face. On the whole, Angel Grove was a city known for its friendly community, spectacular views, and general quiet. Although the community remained intact and the spectacular views continued to exist (though changing rather drastically), the quiet nature of Angel Grove would soon be shattered. A new age was coming and the volume wasn't the only aspect to be amplified.

EYEWITNESS PHOTO OF RITA REPULSA ATOP HER BIKE

On August 28, 1993, during a curious classified mission to Earth's moon, two astronauts stumbled upon a strange container. After opening it, they accidentally unleashed an ancient evil onto our world that would become known as Rita Repulsa, the space witch, and her unsightly gang of galactic goons. Upon their release, a bright flash of light beamed from the surface of the moon followed by an earthquake that erupted across the entire earth. Citizens in Angel Grove, fearing that this was the "big one," ran from their homes and businesses into the streets where they were soon met by the appearance of a towering golden beast of unknown origin. Now classified as Goldar, this extraterrestrial gold-clad warrior towered over the tallest buildings in the humble city. No longer could the truth be denied; alien life existed and we were most certainly not alone.

If it had not been for the appearance of Angel Grove's sudden saviors, the Power Rangers, all would surely have been lost. That mysterious rainbow band of heroes and their Zords triumphantly defeated Goldar and saved the day. While we celebrated their success, the Rangers surely knew that their job was far from over. Upon his defeat, Goldar fled back to the moon and would return time and time again, always to be thwarted by the efforts of our Mighty Morphin Power Rangers.

Overnight the story of the Power Rangers' extraordinary powers and courage spread around the globe. Quickly becoming a worldwide sensation, their exploits were well documented. But this is not a book about the Power Rangers. They are not the focus of the volume that you currently hold in your hands. Following this introduction, I have included a (very) brief overview of the Rangers, including speculation on their origins and a rumored history. However, beyond those pages you will find only documentation and research regarding those grotesque and fascinating extraterrestrials that, day after day and year after year, attempted to destroy Angel Grove.

BEYOND THESE PAGES, YOU WILL FIND MONSTERS.

The beings that will be covered in this book are officially known by the government as *extraterrestrial biological entities* or EBEs. Unofficially (yet more popularly) they are known as "Evil Space Aliens." While I, too, enjoy the label Evil Space Aliens, it should be said that it is not entirely accurate. Several of these aliens are, indeed, peaceful beings. Furthermore, some of these creatures were created on our very own planet. And ultimately, some have origins unknown and uncertain to all who dare to inquire. And while that fact may be unbelievable to certain skeptics, you will find that I have gathered specific research to prove this fantastic claim. Over all, one hundred and fifteen of these EBEs battled the Power Rangers between mid-1993 and 1996, a staggering number of close encounters surely never again to be witnessed in such a short span of time.

I began documenting the appearances of these creatures long after the events had taken place. I was far too young at the time to have comprehended what was actually occurring. And while I do remember seeing attacks by Tengas and more than one appearance of Goldar on the nightly news, I was far more fascinated than frightened. As I grew older I began searching old, yellowed newspapers and magazines for snapshots and eyewitness reports. I scoured the internet for fuzzy video footage shot on old handheld cameras and news stories recorded onto countless VHS tapes. And after interviewing hundreds of citizens and their children who have lived in Angel Grove all their life, I found myself without adequate resources to complete a well-rounded book.

One afternoon, after several long weeks of further searching and finding nothing, I decided to attend the annual Halloween Costume Party at the Angel Grove Youth Center. I threw together a poorly constructed Frankenstein's monster costume and headed downtown.

Once I arrived, I enjoyed a smoothie or two and danced for several minutes before being distracted by the appearance of the finest robot costume I had ever seen. Seeing that the "robot" was also seemingly apart from the crowd, I decided that perhaps this was an opportune time to strike up a conversation of my own. I introduced myself and a voice from within the carefully crafted costume introduced himself as Al. Off the dance floor, we quickly struck up a conversation about the weather, the party, and, eventually, the noted history of invasions in the city. I trod carefully, not wanting to seem like a fanatic, when Al launched passionately into his own thoughts regarding the events. Our chat must have lasted an hour or two. By the time we'd decided to call it a night, the Youth Center was about to close. We shook hands, and Al congratulated me on the progress I had achieved in my research. He soon left ahead of me with the promise of good things to come.

When I returned home that night and sat down at my desk, I was surprised to discover a small disc to which was attached a note. The note read: *Pursuit of truth and knowledge is most admirable. I hope this helps, Mr. Frankenstein.* The note was signed simply *Al*, and it wasn't until poring through the disc's contents that I discovered that the robot at the party was not a costumed citizen at all. That robot, whom I now know as Alpha 5, had served alongside the Power Rangers for many years and had compiled on that disc a vast amount of information, previously unknown to humankind, regarding the alien encounters in Angel Grove!

ALPHA 5 AT HIS FIRST HALLOWEEN PARTY, 1993

Alpha 5 had compiled an impressively vast stockpile of information recovered from the Command Center surveillance footage, stolen Moon Palace recordings (accessed covertly over several years), and various satellites orbiting Earth. I spent weeks reviewing the data—photos, video clips, in-depth details of the monsters' origins, and, ultimately, all the information I needed to complete this book.

I hope you enjoy it, and remember, always keep your eyes to the sky, or else you might find yourself on the underside of an oversize golden gargoyle toe.

THE POWER RANGERS
ANGEL GROVE'S HOMETOWN HEROES

RANGERS POSING FOR THE PRESS ON POWER RANGERS DAY

WHEN THE POWER RANGERS FIRST ARRIVED IN ANGEL GROVE ON THAT LATE AUGUST DAY, NO ONE COULD HAVE IMAGINED THAT THEY WOULD SOON CALL ANGEL GROVE THEIR HOME.

Their first appearance was preceded by what some have described as "five separate beams of colored light" soaring over the mountains at the edge of the city. Red, yellow, blue, pink, and black. These were the shades that shrouded our heroes in the biggest mystery of all—who are the Power Rangers?

In appearance, the Power Rangers are humanoid in form, of average height, and well built. Those who have been personally rescued by a Ranger have stated in nearly all cases that the voice from within the helmet "definitely" sounded human. While I have my doubts that these super-beings are, indeed, human, there are those who are sure of it and who have, for many years, conceived countless plans and schemes to try and unmask the helmeted heroes. However unsuccessful their attempts were, Eugene "Skull" Skullovitch and Farkas "Bulk" Bulkmeier have stood by their claims that the Power Rangers are human and that they might have even been students at Angel Grove High.

When asked who they suspected, the conspiracy-minded duo turned my question around on me and asked me the same question. Needless to say, that conversation did not get far nor successfully convince me that the Rangers are humans. The documents I received from Alpha 5 exclude any entries of data pertaining to the Rangers' identities. Any photos that might have existed of them out of their suits are not present.

METALLIC ARMOR
SHIMMERING SHIELDS

The Rangers' Metallic Armor was created by Alpha 5 and Zordon to combat the Tenga Warriors brought to Earth by Rito Revolto and later commanded by Master Vile. While the armor gave a shimmering sheen to the Rangers' familiar uniforms, it also granted them enhanced speed and strength along with more durability and resistance to injury. On several occasions, the armor has been seen deflecting enemy fire as well. According to Alpha 5's files, the Metallic Armor is powered by the Morphin Grid and can only be used for a limited time.

While it may be impossible (as of now) to pinpoint the identities of the Power Rangers, I can confidently claim that their powers originate from a galaxy far from our own. Alpha 5's files indicate that the Rangers' powers originally came from Power Coins, conduits for ancient energies drawn from prehistoric dinosaurs given to them by the mighty and powerful Zordon, the Rangers' mentor. These Power Coins are held within a device called a Morpher that each of the Rangers wears on their belt. Alpha's information also spoke of a "Morphin Grid" that aids the Rangers in their powers and abilities, but the science involved in the data-dump was beyond my understanding and, considering this is a general overview, I will not be attempting an overly ambitious description.

Resting in a holster on each Ranger's left hip is a standard issue sidearm known as a Blade Blaster. These weapons are used for close encounters and have been documented to successfully hold back foes. While often used, the Blade Blasters are occasionally holstered when vanquishing a foe calls for a stronger deterrent. For times such as these, each of the Rangers is equipped with their own specialized weapon. The Red Ranger wields the Power Sword, the Black Ranger possesses the Power Axe (with the ability to become a personal, handheld cannon), the Blue Ranger holds the Power Lance (able to split into two parts), the Yellow Ranger employs dual Power Daggers, and the Pink Ranger's personal firearm is the Power Bow. Powerful when used separately, all five weapons can be combined to form the Power Blaster that fires a deadly burst of energy often effective against rampaging monsters.

Outside of each Ranger's mastery of martial arts and awesome weaponry, their most powerful resource in

battle is their command of the massive Zords. These magnificent vehicles seemingly rested dormant beneath the earth's surface before their arrival brought about by the Power Rangers. When called upon, these prehistoric machines are combined effortlessly into what we now know is called a Megazord. It is with this colossal mechanism that the Rangers have slain even their most daunting foe. The Dinozords, being the most memorable of all the Zords, were sadly destroyed, only to be refashioned into new and equally powerful Thunderzords. The Thunderzords were, too, replaced after a particularly shocking and heartbreaking ordeal, which has been covered widely on the news, both televised and written.

Before moving on from the Power Rangers, I should mention that while the Rangers began as five, they very quickly became six. Citizens of Angel Grove will remember the day that the deadly Dragonzord tore through the

coastline, nearly flattening the shipping docks at the edge of the city. Commanding the Dragonzord was a terrifying sight: the Green Ranger, a more-than-worthy foe of the Power Rangers. Citizens of Angel Grove are altogether thankful for whatever forces brought him back onto the side of our heroes.

SHARK CYCLES
TRANSPORTATION WITH TEETH

These incredible vehicles were crafted out of the fossilized fin of a great prehistoric shark and offer the Power Rangers a speedy companion in their fight against evil. Swift and powerful, the spirit of that great shark resides within them and, according to Zordon, will always serve the Rangers well. Alpha 5 was responsible for outfitting the Shark Cycles with various battle features.

THE ZORDS

MIGHTY MORPHIN MACHINES

Throughout the course of the alien encounters in Angel Grove, the citizens of the city witnessed not only monsters but also large mechanical warriors who frequently defeated the invading forces.

RED

TYRANNOSAURUS DINOZORD

RED DRAGON THUNDERZORD

APE NINJAZORD

BLACK

MASTODON DINOZORD

LION THUNDERZORD

FROG NINJAZORD

YELLOW

SABERTOOTH TIGER DINOZORD

GRIFFIN THUNDERZORD

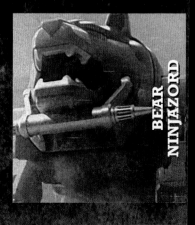

BEAR NINJAZORD

These colossal machines piloted by the Power Rangers are known as Zords and wield awesome powers and abilities. While the Power Rangers rarely changed in appearance, their Zords came and went with frequency over the years. Of course, given the stresses of battling monsters that weighed in at around several tons, it's understandable that new Zords would eventually be required. Over the following pages I've included a reference guide to the various Zords as they're mentioned throughout the collection of encounters.

BLUE

TRICERATOPS DINOZORD

UNICORN THUNDERZORD

WOLF NINJAZORD

PINK

PTERODACTYL DINOZORD

FIREBIRD THUNDERZORD

CRANE NINJAZORD

GREEN/WHITE

DRAGONZORD

WHITE TIGERZORD

FALCONZORD

THE MEGAZORDS
Tougher Together

DINOZORD SYSTEM

The original Zords of the Mighty Morphin Power Rangers met their perceived end during the arrival of Lord Zedd on the moon. During these events, Zedd, furious with the Power Rangers' resilience, opened up a chasm in the earth's crust, which seemingly sent the loyal Dinozords to their molten death. With the retreat of the Dragonzord to the ocean for protection, Alpha 5 managed to recover enough of the Dinozords to create new and more powerful Thunderzords.

THUNDERZORD SYSTEM

The Thunderzords, forged from the remains of the nearly destroyed Dinozords, served the Power Rangers well. Unfortunately, like the Dinozords before them, the Thunderzords met an untimely end at the hands of another maniac from the moon—Rito Revolto. The final destruction of their Thunderzords would lead the Rangers on a quest for other Zords, far more ancient and powerful than they had previously known.

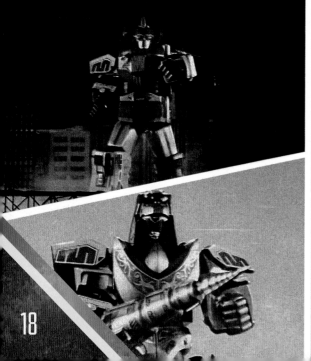

NINJAZORD SYSTEM

After traveling to the Temple of Power, the Rangers were introduced to a being known as Ninjor. Ninjor granted the six Rangers not only new Zords but new Ninja powers as well. Further information regarding this "Ninja Quest" is unknown. Alpha 5's data does not go into much detail regarding the specifics of these newfound Ninjazords or their origin. The Ninjazords were last seen before the events involving the Alien Rangers. Their current whereabouts are unknown.

SHOGUNZORDS SYSTEM

Wielding the Fire Saber, the Shogun Megazord is one of the most powerful combined forces utilized by the Power Rangers. Originally used by Lord Zedd against the Power Rangers, these ancient Zords were eventually taken back by the heroes of Angel Grove and used in the fight against evil. The Shogunzords combine to form the Shogun Megazord, which succeeded in destroying countless foes in its short tenure.

ZORDON OF ELTAR AND ALPHA 5
THE TIME WARP AND THE AUTOMATON

ALPHA IN THE COMMAND CENTER

THE AMOUNT OF INFORMATION I WAS GIVEN REGARDING ZORDON IS SMALL, YET REMARKABLY REVEALING.

Originating from a planet called Eltar located in a galaxy far from our own, Zordon was once a warrior not unlike the Power Rangers. Several thousand years ago Zordon fought against the forces of darkness in the galaxy. One of those forces was the same Rita Repulsa who reappeared after ten thousand years trapped in a space dumpster on our moon. Little is known about their interactions or how they came to be near Earth, but I speculate that a war was fought between the two. And while Zordon was successful in defeating Rita (for the time being), he, too, suffered consequences.

In the image supplied to me by Alpha 5, it is clear that Zordon is no longer flesh and blood like most intelligent organisms in the galaxy. Details suggest that he is, in fact, trapped inside of a time warp where his existence continues living in containment. This containment unit, a large vertical tube of some sort, stands within the central chamber of the Command Center, which lies hidden in the mountains. The location of this Command Center is unknown. (Though I would not be surprised if some sort of high-tech camouflage is utilized to hide the immense structure from prying eyes.)

It is from this Command Center that the

Power Rangers operate. Whether or not they live there is unknown. The single image provided of the Command Center displays the sizable architecture, so it's easy to imagine that rooms of all sorts exist within. Only the existence of the Control Center at the heart of the Command Center can be confirmed. It is in this Control Center that Zordon's chamber stands and where his all-seeing viewing globe looks out over the world, scanning for signs of danger and deceit. This very viewing globe was utilized by Alpha 5 in capturing many images that you will see scattered throughout this book.

ZORDON WITHIN THE TIME WARP

Within the Control Center, Alpha 5 is in charge of maintaining the central control console. Within this console he is able to teleport the Rangers to and from any number of locations, analyze multitudes of data, keep an eye on the charging and repair of Zords, and receive warning of new threats via a diamond-shaped siren that emits a squealing sound. Although seemingly unimportant in an analysis of new life-forms from far away galaxies, Alpha 5 also added that he's been a long-standing fan of hip-hop and, at one point, short-circuited the console by playing his music loudly.

Beyond his love of hip-hop and his passion for dance, Alpha 5 serves Zordon as an automated assistant. While he is a robot, Alpha included a distinction in his notes stating that he is very much alive and experiences a full range of emotions. He states that he is from a planet called Edenoi and was created many thousands of years ago by the wise ruler of that planet, King Lexian.

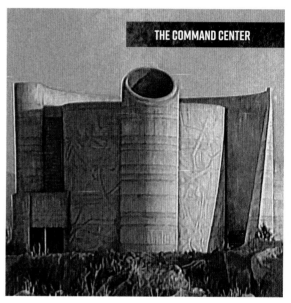

THE COMMAND CENTER

Although the mighty Power Rangers stand prominently in the spotlight and have been applauded and celebrated year after year for their heroism, I believe it is important that the world recognize the everyday heroism of Zordon and Alpha 5. If not for Zordon, we would not have the Power Rangers to protect us. If not for Alpha 5, one can imagine many of the Power Rangers' plans would have fallen apart. Zordon may be an alien from a faraway galaxy and Alpha 5 may be an abnormal android, but at the end of the day, they stand as heroes right next to our Power Rangers.

TITANUS, TOR, AND NINJOR
MIGHTY MORPHIN ALLIES

TITANUS
BRACHIOSAURUS CARRIERZORD

TOR
TURTLE SHUTTLEZORD

A powerful ally and equally important friend in the battle against evil, Titanus is an independent Zord. Titanus is able to merge with the Mega Dragonzord, forming the Dino Ultrazord. This Zord can also combine with various Zords to form both the Ninja Ultrazord and the Shogun Ultrazord.

Similar to Titanus, Tor is an independent Zord and ally to the Power Rangers. Not much is known about Tor's origins, though some data suggests that Tor was created by Zordon from a normal Earth turtle and some other mysterious power source. Most often utilized as a shuttle of sorts, Tor is capable of holding the Rangers' combined Zords to form the Thunder Ultrazord. Tor's most astounding achievement was the shielding of the Rangers' Zords against the might (and weight) of Lord Zedd's Serpentera.

Before profiling Angel Grove's most notorious invaders, monsters, and vile mutations, it is important to briefly note a few more important allies and Zords.

LEGENDARY NINJA MASTER

Ninjor is possibly the Power Rangers' most reliable and significant ally. After losing their powers and Zords following a battle with Rito Revolto, the Power Rangers sought out the Temple of Power. There they met Ninjor, holder of the new Ninja Power Coins and Ninjazords, and convinced him of their commitment to protecting Earth against evil. Reluctant at first, Ninjor recognized the truth in the Power Rangers and granted them their new Power Coins and Zords. Following their initial encounter, Ninjor would return to fight alongside the Rangers on countless occasions, often arriving on a puffy white cloud gliding through the sky.

THE HOT SPOTS

ANGEL GROVE YOUTH CENTER

Arguably one of the most popular spots for both youngsters and monsters in the city, the Angel Grove Youth Center has seen the likes of the Frankenstein Monster, Dramole, and the Pudgy Pig waltz through its doors (or come up from beneath the floorboards).

Opened and, until 1997, owned by the ever-pleasant Ernie, the Gym and Juice Bar is a landmark that still stands and has been witness to many a fascinating and fearful encounter.

ANGEL GROVE PARK

The Angel Grove Park has been accustomed to countless attacks and battles over the years. Putties were often witnessed near playgrounds and popular picnic spots. Several statues throughout the park have also attracted certain dangerous beings, either brought to Earth or

made from the very monuments themselves. When rampaging monsters are rather sparse, the park is certainly the most pleasant spot to spend a day in order to avoid the concrete and steel of the small yet bustling city.

THE MOUNTAINS

Surrounding one side of Angel Grove are an array of mountains that have, fortunately, been the stomping grounds of much monster mayhem. With caves and crevices aplenty, it's best not to journey into the shadowy peaks without some form of protection—you never

know what you'll find. While encounters generally begin either in the park or in downtown Angel Grove, the Power Rangers, always looking to protect citizens, make sure to move most of their fights to the mountains.

THE SHORE

The summers in Angel Grove are known for being hot and humid. When the temperature soars, citizens head to the ocean shore bordering the opposite side of the city. While encounters and sightings at the seaside are far less frequent than those in the mountains

or park, it's smart to keep one eye on what might be lurking beneath the waves.

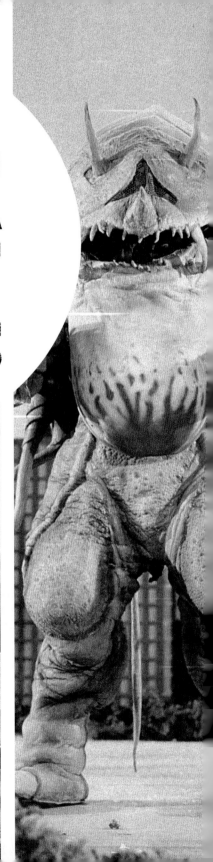

YEAR ONE

(1993–1994)

THE ARRIVAL

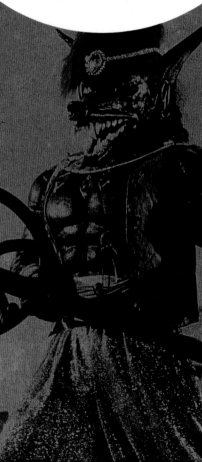

PART ONE

THE MAIN THREAT

RITA REPULSA

Alias (Nickname)

Majestic Maven of Malevolence,
Evil One, Your Putridness, etc.

Known Abilities

Magic Staff (Wand),
Army of Putties
and Monsters

ALPHA 5'S MENACE METER

▶ Run. Please, run. ◀

Take Cover.

Keep Away.

Mostly Harmless.

"Ahh! After ten thousand years, I'm free! It's time to conquer Earth!"

WICKED, VILE, RUDE, AND POSSESSING AN ATTITUDE UNLIKE ANYTHING THE PEOPLE OF EARTH HAD EVER SEEN, RITA REPULSA WAS A DESTRUCTIVE FORCE OF EVIL.

She relished the most heinous and horrific activities, took joy in seeing earthlings suffer, and had a particular panache for conceptualizing crazy creatures beyond our wildest imaginations. So, how did she come to be on our beloved moon?

A pair of well-intentioned astronauts on an unknown expedition across the surface of our celestial neighbor stumbled upon an artifact that they neither understood nor believed could be dangerous. This artifact, now known as a "space dumpster," had rested on the surface of the moon for over ten thousand years, where it had remained sealed. These astronauts were not aware of this information and upon finding the top of the container, thrust it open. Thus began the very saga that you will find throughout the pages of this book.

Upon opening the space dumpster, the astronauts were thrown back by a furious force that emerged from the cratered container. In front of them stood Rita Repulsa, Goldar, Finster, and Rita's ever-reliant henchmen, Squatt and Baboo. Having been locked up in the cramped space for all those years, the crazy creatures that emerged were thirsting for mayhem and madness. Little is known about how Rita and her fellow intergalactic invaders were captured in the container. It appears that Zordon played a big part in making sure that they remained there forever. Perhaps Zordon did not foresee the fault of man in his long-term plan.

RITA OCCASIONALLY MADE HER PRESENCE KNOWN ON EARTH BY APPEARING IN THE SKIES ATOP HER MAGICAL BICYCLE OR STANDING UPON A LEVITATING CHUNK OF ROCK.

However, Repulsa ultimately relied on Squatt and Baboo to take care of her earthbound deeds. The two blue, blubbering helpers, constantly belittled by their mistress, always fell in line behind her increasingly absurd ideas. Goldar, never quite interested in Rita's rule, often questioned the moon maiden's ideas. Rita's true strength seemingly rested upon her respectful creator of monsters—Finster. It is my opinion, after reviewing Alpha 5's files, that Finster, though quiet and largely uninvolved, was the true brains behind Rita's revolution.

Frequently experiencing violent

BAD IS BEAUTIFUL
RITA'S EGO

Although the "compliments" given to her may appear to be insults here on Earth, Rita Repulsa heavily relies on remarks from her minions regarding her "awfulness." In fact, Rita's appearance and presence among the monsters was so important to her that, upon escaping the space dumpster for the second time, Finster coated Rita's face in a Moon Mud Mask that rejuvenated her aged appearance and restored her looks. Apparently, she doesn't look a day over eleven thousand.

headaches and being consistently surprised by her losses, Rita Repulsa always upheld her dream to be the "queen of everything." Along with her strong belief that "bad is beautiful," Rita Repulsa also successfully led the longest string of consecutive attacks against the Power Rangers and our planet.

RITA'S STAFF MAKES LANDFALL

Rita's insane imagination and Finster's fearless creativity gave birth to beings such as Pudgy Pig, Pine-Octopus, Spit Flower, Fang, and Polluticorn. And when the minions and monsters sent to Earth faltered in their attempts at subduing the Power Rangers, Rita would cast down her magic staff, making them grow taller than the surrounding city and landscape. By far, Rita's greatest achievement was her destructive display of control over the power of the Green Ranger and his dangerous Dragonzord. In the end, Rita Repulsa remains Earth's first and most frightening invader. On several occasions, she nearly crippled the collective power of the Mighty Morphin Rangers. More than once she created a monster whose frightful potential was felt around the globe. And from the Moon Palace, a mere 238,900 miles away from our home, Rita Repulsa plotted and produced more monsters than any of her successors.

REPULSISCOPE
HER ALL-SEEING EYE

While Rita's successor, Lord Zedd, would utilize his own gaze to view the events on Earth, the Moon Sorceress relies upon more practical means. Rita's "Repulsiscope," an oversize telescope of sorts, allows the Dark Queen unlimited access to the lives of the citizens of Angel Grove. Later removed upon Zedd's occupation, the Repulsiscope would eventually be returned following the wedding of the two overlords.

DESIGNATION
GOLDAR

Alias (Nickname)
Brass-Plated Baboon
Known Abilities
Enhanced Strength,
Unbreakable Armor,
Access to the
Dark Dimension

ALPHA 5'S MENACE METER

▶ Run. Please, run. ◀

Take Cover.

Keep Away.

Mostly Harmless.

34

> ## "You are only human, and no mere human is a match for Goldar!"

PERHAPS THE STRONGEST SOLDIER IN RITA'S ARMY, GOLDAR HAD THE DISTINCT HONOR OF BEING THE FIRST OF RITA'S EVIL SPACE ALIENS TO INVADE EARTH.

On the day now known as "The Day of the Dumpster," Goldar made his alien presence known when he appeared in the city following a violent earthquake presumably caused by the return of evil on the moon. Citizens of the city were treated to the terrifying sight of the gold-clad, humanoid ape when he appeared in central Angel Grove with a platoon of never-before-seen foot soldiers. It wasn't until his towering arrival (temporarily grown by Rita's magic) over the city's tallest buildings that eyewitnesses got a glimpse of his hideous fangs and glowering red eyes. From that day forward, Angel Grove would witness Goldar's awesome power again and again.

Goldar quickly became a face to fear in Angel Grove. Like birds taking flight before a storm, the appearance of the sword-wielding beast usually meant a bigger, meaner monster was on the way. More often than not, the Power Rangers would quickly arrive to attack their foe only to find that his momentary defeat would bring about a greater threat. In addition, Goldar was also involved in nearly every abduction reported within the city. Though the abductees would often end up in the hands (or claws) of one of Rita's creations, it was generally Goldar who would be tasked with kidnapping the unsuspecting targets.

According to data acquired

by Alpha 5, during Goldar's constant battles with the heroic Power Rangers, he eventually developed a severe distaste for certain members of the mighty team. Specifically, Rita Repulsa's near alliance with Green Ranger set up a rivalry between the two warriors.

IMAGE OF THE DARK DIMENSION, ACQUIRED BY ALPHA 5 FROM MOON PALACE DATA

EARTHLINGS MAY NATURALLY ASSUME THAT GOLDAR MUST BE FAVORED BY THE EMPRESS OF EVIL. ACCORDING TO ALPHA 5'S DATA, THIS IS NOT ENTIRELY TRUE AND WHAT IS INDEED FACT IS FAR MORE FASCINATING.

Long before Goldar found himself saddled with Rita and her band of extraterrestrials, the apelike warrior held a much higher and more noble role in Lord Zedd's army of evil. While it is unknown whether or not Goldar served Zedd for a long period of time, this fact has evidently no bearing on his loyalty to the Emperor of Evil. His loyalty was pushed to the limits when he was appointed Rita's general by Lord Zedd, a task

CYCLOPSIS

GOLDAR'S ZORD

An evil War Zord, Cyclopsis appeared in Angel Grove closely following Goldar's arrival. This Zord, piloted by Goldar, was a strong and nearly undefeatable obstacle in the early days of the Power Rangers. Apparently, it was used around ten thousand years ago, prior to Rita and her minions being locked in the space dumpster. Cyclopsis was ultimately defeated after a long battle involving the summoning of Titanus.

that Goldar found to be beneath his abilities and strength.

AS SOON AS LORD ZEDD ARRIVED ON THE MOON AFTER RITA'S FREQUENT FAILURES, GOLDAR SWIFTLY ALIGNED HIMSELF ONCE MORE WITH HIS OLD MASTER.

For Goldar's groveling, Zedd returned to him that which Rita had once taken away—his wings. And so, as Rita was once again cast off into the darkness of space, the golden gargoyle remained perched beside the throne of the new power within the Moon Palace.

IMAGE OF THE DARK DIMENSION, ACQUIRED BY ALPHA 5 FROM MOON PALACE DATA

DARK DIMENSION
PRISON OF FOG

Although not directly created by or belonging to Goldar, the Dark Dimension was often utilized and visited by Rita and Zedd's number one lackey. This Dark Dimension is supposedly a prisonlike place where unfortunate individuals on the wrong end of Zedd and Rita's fury and frustration end up. Here, where many of the Power Rangers have been captured, Goldar serves as an interrogator and intimidator.

DESIGNATION
SCORPINA

Alias (Nickname)
Scorpion Monster

Known Abilities
Boomerang Blade,
Scorpion-Beast
Transformation,
Pet Weaveworm

**ALPHA 5'S
MENACE
METER**

▶ Run. Please, run.

Take Cover.

Keep Away.

Mostly Harmless.

"BEWARE OF SCORPINA'S STING," STATES ALPHA 5'S DATA REGARDING THE NEXT MINION IN RITA'S MENAGERIE OF EXTRATERRESTRIAL ENTITIES.

While appearing to be a normal humanoid female, Scorpina holds a secret ability. Unlike many other monsters who grow to magnificent size by the power of Rita's staff, this seemingly dainty danger grows to become the horrific beast behind her name. This mutation causes Scorpina to turn into a scorpion monster of petrifying potential with an elongated, electrified tail. Earthlings are lucky that the monster only emerged on occasion.

Not seen by Alpha 5 for over ten thousand years at the time of her reappearance, Scorpina wields a sickle-shaped blade that she uses as both sword and boomerang. Scorpina, unlike other moon minions, doesn't solely reside in the Moon Palace; she seems to come and go as she pleases and arrives when she's needed. According to Alpha 5's information, Rita refers to Scorpina as an old friend. Often accompanied by Goldar on malicious missions to Angel Grove, Scorpina has fought the Rangers in hand-to-hand combat and against their Zords in her giant scorpion form. In addition to her mild kinship with Rita, it appears that Scorpina and Goldar share a bond not unlike friendship. Some eyewitnesses have reported the two diabolical wrongdoers seemingly enjoying their time spent together terrorizing the city. This is, of course, speculation, and a wild theory at best.

It's true that Scorpina posed a strong threat to the Power Rangers, once even supplying her own monster (Weaveworm), but her specific set of skills were no longer needed upon Zedd's arrival. Often utilized during Rita's brief reign, Scorpina only appeared once after Zedd took control of the Moon Palace and was never seen again. And though she and Rita were regarded as friends, Scorpina did not attend the wedding of Rita and Zedd.

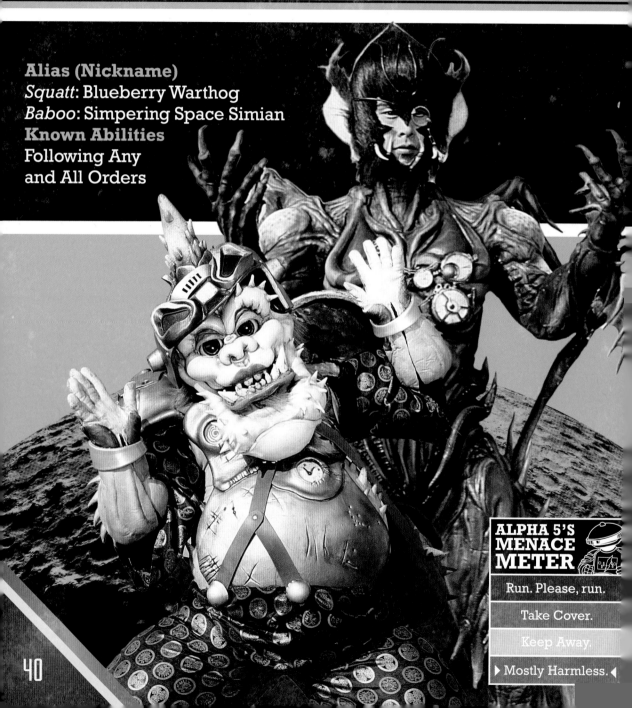

DESIGNATION

SQUATT AND BABOO

Alias (Nickname)
Squatt: Blueberry Warthog
Baboo: Simpering Space Simian
Known Abilities
Following Any
and All Orders

ALPHA 5'S MENACE METER

Run. Please, run.

Take Cover.

Keep Away.

▶ Mostly Harmless. ◀

40

GROVELING, GROTESQUE, AND OFTEN INEFFECTIVE, SQUATT AND BABOO EMERGED FROM THE SPACE DUMPSTER READY TO SERVE THEIR VILE VILLAINESS LOYALLY.

While these two curiosities agreed to do most anything that Rita asked of them, more often than not they failed in their frequent quests or barely managed to complete them.

Even though they are often unable to accomplish many of their given tasks, the two goons do have their redeeming qualities. The monocle-wearing bat being known as Baboo is apparently a master alchemist and successfully created a potion that caused two of the Rangers (Blue and Pink) to display evil characteristics that were later cured. Along with his companion Squatt, Baboo was also partially responsible for the creation of a singular monster known as Shellshock. Squatt, unlike Baboo, seems to be driven by a desire to eat, always prepared for his sudden hunger with a good stock of beetles in his satchel.

Although Rita was full of displeasure toward the two, she continued to utilize them in her schemes against the planet. Oftentimes, the two bewildered blue aliens would be seen side-by-side with Goldar and a gang of Putties as they confronted the Power Rangers in the park or city. Most of the alien encounters reported in the city involve Squatt and Baboo. Curiously enough, Bulk and Skull happened upon the two extraterrestrials on countless occasions.

Squatt and Baboo, not known for their courage, were often used by Rita (and later Lord Zedd) for missions that didn't necessarily need to go right. While their escapades often ended in embarrassment or failure, the two crude blue beings actually succeeded in their tasks enough times to prove to their masters that they had worth, thus securing their place on the moon.

DESIGNATION

FINSTER

Alias (Nickname)
Master of Monsters
Known Abilities
Master Sculptor,
Creator of the
Monster-Matic™

ALPHA 5'S MENACE METER

Run. Please, run.

Take Cover.

Keep Away.

▶ Mostly Harmless.

ASIDE FROM THE GOLD-CLAD GORILLA AND TWO BLUE BUFFOONS, RITA'S TRUE STRENGTH LIES IN THE IMAGINATIVE AND INTELLIGENT MIND OF FINSTER.

The presumed creator of the magnificent yet terrible Monster-Matic™, a machine capable of turning any of Finster's clay creations into reality, Finster is by far the most intelligent member of the motley moon menagerie. The Monster-Matic™ is a small machine situated in Finster's workshop, a place where the dog-like designer works alone and devises extraordinary achievements.

While many of Finster's monsters are created from his expansive intellect, or on commission for Rita Repulsa, the scientist is also known to reference a mysterious and unknown book that supposedly contains documentation and descriptions of monsters throughout the universe. So while Finster creates these monsters from clay on his modest workbench, it can be assumed that many of the monsters sent to Earth are fabrications of real, not fictional, beings beyond our planet.

Finster's work during the reign of Rita was frenzied, packed with tight deadlines from his fearless leader. But while his role was necessary during this time, the arrival of Lord Zedd signaled the end of Finster's renaissance. Lord Zedd, wielding far greater power than Rita Repulsa, simply utilized his Z-Staff, which could conjure a monster simply by pointing it at an object on Earth and casting a spell. Zedd's means for monster construction were far more efficient in the eyes of the evil extraterrestrials on the moon and, therefore, Finster was more or less "benched" during the Emperor of Evil's occupation.

Alias (Nickname)
Clay Brain(s)
Known Abilities
Super Durability,
Never-Ending Supply

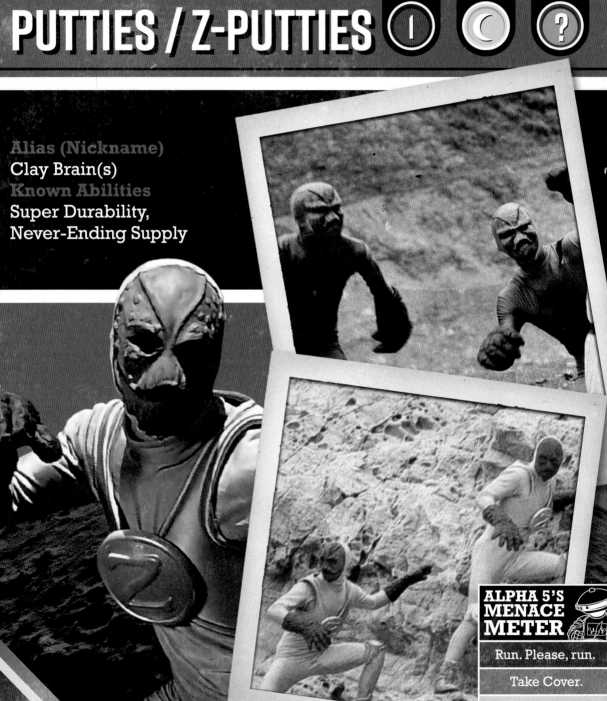

ALPHA 5'S MENACE METER

Run. Please, run.

Take Cover.

▶ Keep Away. ◀

Mostly Harmless.

EVERY SINGLE CITIZEN OF ANGEL GROVE IS FAMILIAR WITH THESE PESTERING PATROLLERS FROM THE MOON PALACE. THE PUTTIES, ALSO KNOWN AS THE PUTTY PATROL, ARE EXPENDABLE AND OBNOXIOUS OBJECTS OF FINSTER'S CREATION.

Formed inside the Monster-Matic™, the Putties serve as either a distraction or the first line of defense before Rita's real plan becomes apparent. More often than not, these gray goons are accompanied by Goldar. Not only has Goldar commanded a platoon of the underwhelming underlings, but a slew of Rita's other monstrous maniacs have also been accompanied by their small army.

Through countless eyewitness testimonies, I have come to the conclusion that Putties are viewed as less of a threat than most beings from the moon. But that is not their primary purpose. The purpose of the Putty is to distract the Power Rangers, aid in abductions, or assist in other equally evil events requiring extra hands. In fact, the threat of the Putties was so minimal that when Lord Zedd arrived and took dominion over the Moon Palace, he made changes to the previously failed flunkies.

With his dark magic, the Monarch of the Moon cast forth a new league of lackeys called Z-Putties. These new frantic flunkies gained not only a costume change, but also enhanced strength and speed. Zedd's new Z-Putties caught the Power Rangers off guard in their debut battle, but the Rangers quickly discovered a key weakness within the stooges. When hit precisely in the center of their chest where Zedd's "Z" was displayed, the new Putties simply burst into small clay bits that blew away in the breeze. Despite this known weakness, Lord Zedd was not discouraged from further use of the clay-brained creatures.

PART TWO

EVIL SPACE ALIENS: MANUFACTURED ON THE MOON

DESIGNATION
BONES

YEAR	ORIGIN	TYPE
①	☾	❓

Alias (Nickname)
n/a

Known Abilities
Optical Energy Blasts, Leaping, Disassemble and Reassemble at Will

THE APPEARANCE OF THE SECOND EVIL SPACE ALIEN IN ANGEL GROVE WAS

preceded by a display of rainbow-colored lights above the city. Soon after, Bones appeared in the local amusement park where citizens ran in terror of the cloaked skeletal being. After setting ablaze a gaming booth with fiery beams shot from his eye sockets, Bones was also seen taking an enjoyable ride on the merry-go-round. It was at this point that the Power Rangers confronted their foe. Without any warning, Bones pulled his head from his shoulders, tossed it through the air, and vanished once again. The skull hung in the air for a moment before beginning to spin. Soon afterward, the Power Rangers and the skull vanished. Information provided by Alpha 5 reveals that the Rangers were transported to a "time warp" where they battled Bones and his Skeleton Warriors, before ultimately defeating the skeletal being by tossing his skull into a fiery pit of lava. Rita responded by sending a giant knight down to Earth, who was almost immediately destroyed upon the arrival of the mighty Zords. Not enough is known about the knight to justify its own documentation.

DESIGNATION
MIGHTY MINOTAUR

YEAR  ORIGIN TYPE

Alias (Nickname)
Most-Menacing
Minotaur
Known Abilities
Unbreakable
Shield, Mace, Horn
Energy Blast

THE ANGEL GROVE INDUSTRIAL WASTE SITE IS ONE OF THE FEW BLEMISHES ON THE

beautiful landscape of the glowing city. It was Rita's intention to pollute Earth, starting with the unpopular industrial site, yet it is unclear how her chosen monster fit into that plan.

Following the appearance of Putties at the waste site, the Mighty Minotaur appeared and was met by the Black, Red, and Blue Rangers. Pulling their Blade Blasters, the Rangers fired at the creature known only from myth and were surprised to have the blasts deflected back at them by the brute's shield.

The Minotaur, once merely human size, grew to an alarming height with the help of Rita's spell, towering over the mountains. The Rangers called upon their ever-reliable Zords, and a furious battle ensued. Each of the Zords took a shot at the Minotaur with its own specialized arsenal but could not take the beast alone. Even combined, the Zords remained ineffective and the Power Rangers retreated. The Minotaur returned to his original size, where he was met by Power Rangers. Quickly, the Rangers proved the power of teamwork by combining their weapons and forming the Power Blaster. And in one quick bolt, the blaster reduced the growling Minotaur to a pint-size puff of smoke.

49

DESIGNATION
KING SPHINX

Alias (Nickname)
n/a
Known Abilities
Magical Teleporting Wings, Flame-Firing Staff

THE INITIAL ENCOUNTER WITH THE MONSTER KNOWN AS KING SPHINX IS ONE OF THE MORE

curious events to be witnessed in Angel Grove. Several bystanders reported that Squatt and Baboo had been waiting on the bleachers surrounding the Children's Theater before the attack began. Soon after, both Putties and the Power Rangers appeared and began to battle.

King Sphinx arrived and quickly did away with the Pink Ranger with his extraordinary wings. I'm led to believe that the gusts of wind generated by King Sphinx transport other beings. Where these victims of Sphinx's wind are sent remains a mystery. The Black Ranger, too, fell victim to King Sphinx's wings.

Angered by the loss of two teammates, the Red Ranger charged the Sphinx and disappeared alongside the furious foe. Apparently, King Sphinx teleported himself and the Red Ranger to the mountains, where Goldar was waiting. There the two beasts attacked the lone Ranger and, fearing defeat from his Blade Blaster, Goldar and King Sphinx received Rita's spell and grew to towering heights.

During the battle, the Red Ranger's compatriots arrived, and together they formed the Megazord. It was then that King Sphinx was ultimately defeated.

GNARLY GNOME

YEAR ORIGIN TYPE

Alias (Nickname)
Bucko
Known Abilities
**Hypnotic Accordion,
Invisibility,
Garden Hoe**

THIS NEXT ENCOUNTER IS PARTICULARLY CHILLING IN ITS DETAILS. DANCE CLASS AT THE

Youth Center had just ended when a strange apparition appeared outside the Juice Bar. The students exited the building and were met by this creature, now known as the Gnarly Gnome. Before they even knew what was happening, the students were hypnotized by the Gnome's magical accordion.

The hypnotized children followed the Gnome to a cave in the mountains. There they were trapped, the entrance of the cave blocked and the hypnotizing music of the accordion keeping them under the Gnome's spell. Later reports uncovered by local law enforcement paint a curious picture: Within the cave was a large feast covering an equally large table. Alpha 5's data further indicates that the children were ordered to dance while the Gnarly Gnome enjoyed his vast spread of food.

The Power Rangers soon arrived and nearly defeated their foe. If Rita's staff hadn't intervened, the battle would have been over quickly. And yet, even after the Gnome was grown, he proved to be weak. Once the Zords arrived, the gnarly beast was defeated with a swift swipe of the Megazord's Power Sword. The children, of course, were returned to the city unharmed and largely unaware of what had transpired.

PUDGY PIG

YEAR	ORIGIN	TYPE
I		

Alias (Nickname)
Porker
Known Abilities
Insatiable Appetite,
Transporting Snout
Vortex

THE ANGEL GROVE YOUTH CENTER WAS HOSTING A CULTURAL FOOD FESTIVAL WHEN A SUDDEN AND

disruptive food fight was instigated by the delinquents known as Bulk and Skull. The Food Fest was soon to be the all-you-can-eat buffet for one unwelcome guest. The Pudgy Pig was first spotted in an alleyway downtown, wildy shoving his face into trash cans. Soon after, he teleported and wound up in Angel Grove Park, where he unkindly disrupted a quaint picnic between friends by diving onto the blanket and devouring all the snacks. Next, he appeared at the Urkupina Market, a local grocery store, where he ate every last piece of food, except for spicy edibles.

It was after making a mess of those locations that Pudgy disrupted the Food Festival. The Power Rangers finally had a run-in with the piggy pest wherein the creature ate their weapons one after the other. The Pudgy Pig would later appear at the M. G. R. Food Packing Plant outside Angel Grove, where he would be dispatched by the Power Rangers after being offered spicy food, which forced him to vomit up the Ranger weapons he had earlier devoured. With these same weapons, the Power Rangers defeated the ravenous Pig. According to Alpha 5, Zordon had estimated that if not stopped, Pudgy would have swallowed all Earth's food supply in less than forty-eight hours.

CHUNKY CHICKEN

YEAR	ORIGIN	TYPE

Alias (Nickname)
n/a
Known Abilities
Sword-Like
Garden Shears,
Teleportation

ACCORDING TO ALPHA 5'S FILES, THIS FEISTY FOWL WAS SENT TO EARTH BY RITA REPULSA

with the sole purpose of abducting a child who could be utilized to open a chest containing ancient Power Eggs. These Power Eggs, created many millions of years ago, hold unlimited cosmic potential. To ensure the safety of the powerful eggs, a spell was cast upon the chest, which, without the touch of an innocent child, would not open.

After opening the chest (with the forced help of the abducted child, Maria), Goldar, Squatt, and Baboo fled with the eggs. They were soon hit by a blast from the Power Blaster, which knocked the eggs from their grasp, and into the sea.

Chunky Chicken escaped and was later found in central Angel Grove. Maria was found, unharmed, hanging from a rope. The feathered freak flew about his prey and cut the rope as soon as the Power Rangers arrived. Not wasting a moment, the Rangers summoned their Zords and, at the last second, caught Maria before she could hit the ground. Rita, who had arrived minutes earlier on her flying bicycle, threw down her wand, thus granting the chicken growth. A swift swipe of the Power Sword, after a brief scuffle, destroyed the rotten egg, leaving Angel Grove safe for another day.

Alias (Nickname)
Bug-Eyed Freak

Known Abilities
Large Main Eye
(Entrance to
Another Realm),
Projectile Fireballs,
Intelligence
Absorption

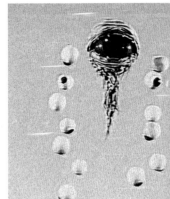

MOST DEFINITELY NOT A SIGHT FOR SORE EYES, EYE GUY STOOD OUT AS ONE OF RITA'S

superior creations. Originally utilized in an attack on the planet Rigel Two, Eye Guy's specialty is kidnapping and absorbing the intelligence of the smartest beings on any given planet—children.

Eye Guy first appeared as a disembodied, floating eye-stalk. An eyewitness reported that a "weird floating ball" approached a boy sitting at the edge of the lake. A "brilliant beam of light" shot from the eye and the boy disappeared. The eye retreated back to the woods.

Not long after, the Power Rangers encountered Eye Guy, who stood and laughed at them. A battle quickly ensued and the Rangers blew the beast into pieces with their Power Blaster. Eye Guy pulled himself together just in time to deliver a fierce blow, sending the Rangers over a cliff.

They returned, except for the Blue Ranger, who snuck off into the woods, locating the main eye and striking it with his Power Lance. Eye Guy, also facing off against the other Rangers, felt the blow and was weakened considerably. Rita intervened and Eye Guy grew. With their foe no longer at eye level, the Rangers called upon their Zords and destroyed Eye Guy, releasing the abducted child who had been held briefly within another realm.

DESIGNATION
MR. TICKLESNEEZER

YEAR
ORIGIN
TYPE

Alias (Nickname)
Does he really
need one?
Known Abilities
Goody Bottle

THIS CROSS-EYED, ELFISH CREATURE IS BY FAR ONE OF RITA'S MOST CURIOUS CREATIONS.

Through research I came to understand that Mr. Ticklesneezer bears a remarkable resemblance to a popular doll found in many parts of the world. It comes as no surprise that this creature is rumored to have been created from one of those very dolls, belonging to a student at Angel Grove High.

Nearly always giggling, Ticklesneezer didn't seem to understand his role as a mechanism of Rita's attempt at world domination. Ticklesneezer never seemed to intentionally harm the Power Rangers or other citizens of the city—he simply liked to collect things, snatching up any items that he desired and storing them in his Goody Bottle. It even appeared, at one point, that Goldar, Squatt, and Baboo had been sent to look after the elf in order to ensure that he committed dastardly deeds. During his brief time in Angel Grove, Ticklesneezer collected an airplane (midflight), a train, a building, and, on the smaller side, a dirt bike. All of these items were returned to their original size and placed at the foot of the Megazord upon Ticklesneezer's defeat.

55

DESIGNATION
KNASTY KNIGHT

YEAR	ORIGIN	TYPE
1	✦	☻

Alias (Nickname)
Sir Buckethead
Known Abilities
All-Cutting Sword,
Magical Powers,
Flame Projection

ORIGINALLY UTILIZED BY RITA REPULSA ON A PLANET CALLED TARMAC 3, THE KNASTY KNIGHT

proved to be an exceptional swordsman. Summoned to Earth by one of Rita's many spells, this intergalactic champion was given a sword created by Finster (with the help of Squatt and Baboo) in the woods outside Angel Grove. One eyewitness who wished to remain anonymous saw the "dog-looking one" and the "two blue ones" in the woods with an anvil on which they were fashioning a deadly new blade for the ancient warrior.

The Knasty Knight first appeared in these woods in the company of Rita's three minions and the evil witch herself. The Black Ranger was the first on the scene, quickly joined by the other Rangers. While their battle was harsh and their weapons nearly destroyed, the Rangers retaliated against Knasty's attacks, eventually calling upon their Zords and entering a monstrous swordfight of the ages. Towering over the buildings of Angel Grove, the Knight's sword met Megazord metal, eventually shattering under the strength of the ancient Power Sword. And so, with a final slash, the Power Rangers said "nighty-knight" to another armor-clad antagonist.

PINE-OCTOPUS

YEAR	ORIGIN	TYPE

Alias (Nickname)
Pineapple-Face
Known Abilities
Magical
Transfiguration Ray,
Energy Projection,
Terrifying Laughter

CLAIMING TO BE UNBEATABLE, THE PINE-OCTOPUS MONSTER

was one of the Power Rangers' most wonderfully wicked adversaries. During a town fair just outside Angel Grove, Pine-Octopus (under the human-like disguise of "Pineapple the Clown") launched an all-out attack on the citizens in the park. This strange entity even succeeded in turning one girl into a cardboard cutout with his odd and unexpected powers. Supported by a band of clowns turned Putties, Pine-Octopus was capable of unleashing a shower of golden flakes that subatomically transformed any living being into a two-dimensional state when touched. Fortunately, moments after Pineapple the Clown revealed himself to be the true monster that he was (by means of melting and transforming into the Pine-Octopus), the Power Rangers arrived. Quickly evacuating the fair, the Rangers defeated a towering Pine-Octopus and revived those transformed using a simple solution of water.

TERROR TOAD

Alias (Nickname)
Wartsville
Known Abilities
Glowing Tongue,
Large Stomach

BEING DEVOURED BY A MONSTER WAS CERTAINLY NOT THE EXPECTATION OF

the Power Rangers when they signed up for the job. But, unfortunately, most of them met this fate (briefly) while battling the gluttonous Terror Toad. An extraterrestrial amphibian with a second face hiding beneath its neck flaps, the Terror Toad is large, hungry, and quite mean. Its guttural laughter, razor-sharp teeth, and prominent forehead horn make for an exceptional distraction from the Toad's true power—the ability to release a giant, luminescent tongue from its mouth and swallow whole anyone who stands in its way. Before this slobbering toadstool squatter met his defeat at the hands of the Pink Ranger and her powerful bow, Terror Toad proved to be more than capable of aiding Rita in her plans for world domination. After swallowing up the Black, Yellow, Red, and Blue Rangers, the Terror Toad had almost won. Although briefly inconvenienced by an attack by Baboo, the Pink Ranger regained her composure and delivered the final blow, launching in quick succession a barrage of arrows into the Toad's secondary face. The awful amphibian was defeated, releasing all the Power Rangers from his grotesque gut.

MADAME WOE

Alias (Nickname)
Nightmare Queen
Known Abilities
Dimensional
Transport
(via Crown Jewel),
Control of Elements,
Prehensile Braids

MADAME WOE WAS ONE OF THE FIRST UBER-MYSTICAL BEINGS TO BE THROWN INTO THE

ring with the Power Rangers. Her mastery of the elements and control over the sun, the moon, and other natural wonders made her one of their more advanced foes. Called upon by Rita, Woe made her presence known on the bluffs at the edge of Angel Grove overlooking the Pacific Ocean. According to eyewitnesses, Madame Woe appeared to a female student of Angel Grove High named Marge and promptly teleported the unsuspecting pedestrian into another dimension. Alpha 5's information does not reveal much about the dimension to which the student was sent, only that it was a "dark reflection" of our world, filled with fog. Eventually the Power Rangers were alerted to Woe's abduction and pursued her until they themselves were transported to the dark dimension. However, due to their cunning and bravery, the Power Rangers escaped the dimension, saved Marge, and destroyed Woe's Crown Jewel. Needless to say, Madame Woe was never seen again and the Power Rangers stood victorious in their favorite city.

DESIGNATION
SNIZZARD

YEAR	ORIGIN	TYPE

Alias (Nickname)
n/a
Known Abilities
Vicious Leg Cobras,
Energy-Draining
Cobra Arrow

THE SNIZZARD WAS A BIG SNAKE MADE UP OF MANY SMALL SNAKES.

Though created by the fearsome and occasionally genius Finster, this slithering serpent had an obvious weakness—a prominent golden apple perched on the top of its scaly head. Unlike many other monsters, the Snizzard made only one appearance in Angel Grove—near the large fountain in the center of the park. It was at this fountain, soon after its appearance, that the Snizzard would be met by four of the five Power Rangers. Although the Rangers' initial strikes were promising, the monstrous reptile fought ruthlessly, lashing out its tail at the Red Ranger and ultimately launching snakes from its mouth that effortlessly bound the Rangers. For a few moments, the snakes began draining the Rangers' energy and all seemed lost. Fortunately, the Pink Ranger arrived and, after taking out a swarm of Putties with her trusty bow, released the other Rangers by cutting the snakes in half. According to Alpha 5's data, the Snizzard, angered by Pink's heroism, readied the launch of further snakes to attack the newly freed Rangers. Unfortunately for the brute, Pink quickly delivered one final blow with an arrow to the apple, and the Snizzard erupted in a shower of sparks and lightning.

DESIGNATION

DARK WARRIOR

YEAR	ORIGIN	TYPE

Alias (Nickname)
n/a
Known Abilities
Sword, Projectile
Wrist Bombs,
Scythe and Chain

THE SPEED OF A PANTHER, THE WISDOM OF THE AGES,

and the strength of ten angry Octavian Slime Toads were combined in order to make the Dark Warrior, according to Alpha 5's data. What could have been one of Finster's finest creations ultimately failed to accomplish much during its time on Earth. After kidnapping a world-renowned scientist and champion martial artist who was rumored to have developed a successful invisibility formula, the camouflaged combatant tucked the visiting academic away in a mountain cave bordering Angel Grove. The Power Rangers soon found the scientist and rescued him, leading to a fierce face-off with the Dark Warrior against the backdrop of the California mountain range. Fearing failure from the Warrior, Rita once again sent down her wand and made her newest extraterrestrial invader grow to monumental proportions. However, this action would prove less than fruitful for the moon witch. Even while wielding his terrible scythe, the now-gigantic Dark Warrior quickly fell at the swing of the Megazord's blade.

61

DESIGNATION

THE GENIE

Alias (Nickname)
Anubis
Known Abilities
Projectile Spears,
Web Snare,
Drill-Staff

ORIGINATING FROM CANINE FOUR OF THE WOLF'S HEAD GALAXY, THE GENIE, AS HE

is commonly known, was awakened from his lamp by Squatt at the command of Rita. Wielding staggering power, the Genie was predicted to be successful against the Power Rangers. Rita, aware of Zordon's ever-watchful eye, knew that sending the Genie to Earth in his lamp would allow him to go undetected until the moment of his second awakening. The space witch then sent Squatt and Baboo to the park, where they rubbed the lamp, unleashing the Genie on Angel Grove. Soon after the appearance of the Genie, the Power Rangers were sighted in a furious battle against Goldar and the Putties in the industrial district of the city. After their victory, the Rangers arrived in the park, where they were quickly overcome by the powerful abilities of the Genie. For a moment, all seemed lost as Rita made her appearance on Earth and cast her spell, making the Genie grow. Towering over the city, the Genie was soon met by the mighty Megazord. After briefly being caught in the Genie's web snare and nearly impaled by his drill-staff, the Rangers watched as the Genie suddenly evaporated into a cloud of smoke. According to Alpha 5's notes, it was he who was responsible for destroying the Genie's lamp and saving the Power Rangers.

GREEN WITH EVIL
RISE OF THE GREEN RANGER

OFTEN REGARDED AS ONE OF THE MOST SIGNIFICANT SAGAS IN THE HISTORY OF THE MIGHTY MORPHIN POWER RANGERS, THE RISE OF THE *EVIL* GREEN RANGER AND HIS DANGEROUS DRAGONZORD SHOOK THE CITY OF ANGEL GROVE TO ITS CORE.

This event began with an apparent abduction in a back alley within the center of the city. The identity of the abductee is unknown and, presumably, will remain so forever. This odd abduction was supposedly preceded by an attack of the Putty Patrol that ended with the stranger remarkably unharmed. It was then, according to eyewitness statements, that Rita Repulsa herself appeared atop a nearby structure and, with her staff, zapped the innocent abductee with a beam. This otherworldly beam, glowing a brilliant green, caused the individual to disappear in a blinding flash of light.

According to Alpha 5's data, this unknown civilian was transported to the dungeons beneath the Moon Palace, where he was placed in a cocoon-like state. It was over this "cocoon" that Rita chanted her spells and performed a ritual of sorts, which placed the newly created Green Ranger under Repulsa's control. After supplying the abductee with the coveted green Power Coin, Rita released her Green Ranger from his cocoon and sent him to Earth, where he masterfully infiltrated the Command Center. Upon arrival, the Green Ranger secretly slipped a disc into Alpha 5's back, causing

64

a violent malfunction. It should be noted that Alpha 5 recalls that the intrusion on his circuitry was quite painful, and for many months afterward, the friendly automaton feared that his system would never fully recover. Fortunately, his notes confirm that was not the case. Following the corruption of Alpha 5's system and his cries for help, Zordon awoke and attempted to intervene in the Green Ranger's plans. This only seemed to further infuriate the rogue Ranger who, before leaving the Command Center, destroyed the central control panel, leaving Zordon lost in his own dimension, unable to contact the Power Rangers.

RITA'S PLAN HAD ONLY JUST BEGUN. MOMENTS AFTER THE GREEN RANGER HAD INCAPACITATED THE COMMAND CENTER, GOLDAR ARRIVED ON EARTH AND GREW GARGANTUAN IN SIZE, TOWERING OVER THE CITY.

The Rangers speedily arrived at the Command Center to be met with a scene of destruction. They were quickly able to repair Alpha 5 after noticing the invasive disc that had been inserted into his back. With Alpha back online and the Command Center back up and running, the Rangers marched to the mountains with their Zords in order to halt Goldar's intended invasion of the city. Unfortunately, the Power Rangers, seemingly safe inside the Megazord, could not have expected what came next. Suddenly appearing on the mountainside, the Green Ranger launched himself onto the shell of

the Megazord. After forcing his way inside, the evil Green Ranger mangled the controls and launched the piloting Power Rangers from their position. Landing roughly on the ground beneath the Megazord, the Rangers stood face-to-face with their mysterious attacker—another Ranger.

Following this awful attack and a later confrontation with the Green Ranger, the city of Angel Grove was introduced to Scorpina. Appearing in the industrial district on the outskirts of the city, Scorpina arrived with a gang of Putties but was quickly defeated. After Scorpina's failure, Rita again sent a now-gigantic Goldar to combat the ever-resilient Power Rangers. The toppling of several large buildings quickly caused the evacuation of many businesses and other establishments throughout the city.

The Rangers rushed to the beach, where Goldar stood with Scorpina and Rita atop the nearby cliffs. At the edge of one of the cliffs sat a bus containing Bulk and Skull. According to the two witnesses, they had attempted to use the bus to evacuate the city and evade Goldar's deadly path. Unfortunately, they were unsuccessful in their attempt. As the bus teetered on the brink of oblivion, a band of Putties joined by Squatt and Baboo slowly began pushing and shaking the vehicle closer and closer to the edge. Seeing the tiny Rangers beneath him, Goldar began thrusting his sword into the sand surrounding them. In an instant, the bus began to fall, but not before the Power Rangers joined their Zords together. The Megazord appeared and caught the bus in one strong hand, placing it safely on the ground below. Seldom have hostages been taken in the long battle against the moon monsters. This case in particular is notable given the imminent threat of death.

SOON THE SUN WAS ECLIPSED BY RITA'S DARK MAGIC, AND THE MEGAZORD BEGAN TO LOSE POWER, WEAKENED BY THE DARKNESS BLOCKING OUT THE ENERGIZING SOLAR RAYS.

Next up, Rita used her magic to make Scorpina grow, and in so doing, gave the Rangers their first view of her horrific scorpion appearance. Joined by Goldar, this terrifying creature that had once looked like a gold-clad woman warrior stood above the seemingly helpless Power Rangers on the beach. As the sun was eclipsed, the Megazord did fall for a moment before being reenergized by the fateful arrival of the legendary Power Sword, an ancient weapon with untold abilities. And not a moment too soon.

Arriving on the beachfront, the Green Ranger was also blessed with one of Rita's growth spells and found himself facing off against the Megazord along with Goldar and Scorpina. After a furious fight, the Megazord finally fell into a crevice that had cracked open at the edge

of the water. In moments, the Megazord, the only hope the Power Rangers had left, was consumed by lava bubbling up from below. The Power Rangers quickly abandoned the battlefield, fleeing for the Command Center.

According to information obtained by Alpha 5, Rita and her minions celebrated by drinking a concoction made from cranberries and oysters (apparently a favorite of the Dark Queen's). Back on Earth, most citizens of Angel Grove watched slack-jawed as images of Goldar's devastating attack on the city played over and over again on their televisions. No one could have expected what happened next.

THE OCEAN BORDERING THE INDUSTRIAL DISTRICT BEGAN TO CHURN AND BUBBLE, THE FROTH OF SEAWATER LAUNCHING INTO THE AIR AND ONTO LAND.

From under the violent waves rose a terrifying and truly unexpected sight—the Dragonzord. Immediately the towering green and black Zord began its march through the docks, destroying everything in its path. Its giant tail, tipped with a deadly drill, ripped through buildings and warehouses alike as it continued on its path toward the city. Ancient and elusive, the Dragonzord had been called from the murky depths by Rita Repulsa herself, a gift, perhaps, for her Green Ranger. Continuing its onslaught of the city, the Dragonzord strode through the business district where the Green Ranger, standing atop a nearby building, commanded the Zord with his Dragon Dagger, a flute-like weapon that directed the diabolical beast with various frequencies.

Just after the Dragonzord launched a devastating deployment of missiles, the Red

Ranger's Tyrannosaurus Dinozord made its triumphant return and entered into a savage battle. The other Zords soon returned to form the newly recovered Megazord, and with fierceness unlike anything achieved before, the Megazord took hold of the Dragonzord's tail and tossed the terrible Zord into the side of a mountain.

According to Alpha 5, following the defeat of the Dragonzord, the Red Ranger and Green Ranger faced off among the rubble at the base of the mountain. It was during this intense battle that the Red Ranger reportedly succeeded in destroying the Green Ranger's Sword of Darkness, thus freeing the abducted innocent from the spell that had been cast by the moon witch. Filled with deep regret over the damage caused, the Green Ranger decided to defy Rita, joining the Power Rangers and becoming a force for good. While it took time for the people of Angel Grove to let go of their fear of the Green Ranger's Dragonzord, all citizens of the fine city agree that without the subsequent efforts made by the Green Ranger, the city would be worse off. Eventually leading the Power Rangers into their battles against numerous foes over the coming months, the Green Ranger remains a symbol of the power of good and the possibility of change.

DESIGNATION
SHELLSHOCK

Alias (Nickname)
Turtle Soup
Known Abilities
Freeze-Ray,
Go-Beam,
Hidden Head
Cannon

WHILE A STOPLIGHT, A BASEBALL BAT, A TURTLE, AND A CANNON HAVE SEEMINGLY

nothing in common, the appearance of Shellshock disturbs that notion. When Squatt and Baboo secretly decided to create their own monster, the result was one of the strangest creatures ever to have towered over the Angel Grove skyline. Shellshock may not have looked like an effective enemy against the Power Rangers, but it soon proved otherwise. Crafted with Finster's Monster-Matic™ machine, using a combination of seemingly random items (brass knuckles, miniature cannon, a baseball bat, and a pirate's hook hand), this terrible turtle utilized each of its given abilities with astonishing results. While the baseball bat and the hook hand proved to be excellent weapons against the Green Ranger's Dragonzord, Shellshock's ultimate power lay within the stoplight perched on its shell. A flash of the green light would send anyone affected into a fit of ceaseless motion. The red light had a freezing effect on its victims. Even though Shellshock was successful in using most of his abilities against the Power Rangers, he ultimately failed along with Squatt and Baboo in their first (and presumably last) effort to impress the Empress of the Moon.

DESIGNATION

SPIDERTRON

YEAR

ORIGIN

TYPE

Alias (Nickname)
Web-Face
Known Abilities
Trap Webs,
Projectile Sticky
Foam, Explosive
Stingers

THE FOREST SPIRIT STATUE, AN ODD YET CHARMING SIGHT

in the midst of Angel Grove's largest park, was set to be torn down and replaced with a barbecue pit. The statue supposedly holds protective powers that keep the insects and critters of Angel Grove safe. It is no surprise, then, that Rita Repulsa found a way to turn the statue into one of her vile monsters, known as Spidertron. Rita sent this creature to Earth and hid it within a decoy Forest Spirit Statue, the original having been stolen away to the moon. It was the Black Ranger who, after discovering a group of unconscious children in the park, sensed something dangerous was moving within the statue. After the destruction of the statue, Spidertron appeared in all of its eight-armed terror, and a battle ensued between the Black Ranger and the creature. Soon, the other Rangers arrived and found themselves trapped in the appalling arachnid's web. Eventually freed from their captivity, the Rangers fought a fierce battle against Spidertron, which only ended with the blow of the Dragonzord. The true Forest Spirit Statue was returned to Earth and remains standing in the park to this day.

SPIT FLOWER

Alias (Nickname)
One Ferocious Bug
Known Abilities
Power-Draining,
Biting Blossoms,
Eyestalk Beams

FLOWERS WERE RIPPED FROM THEIR RESTING PLACES AND TURNED INTO

ferocious, fang-filled blossoms with an unnatural bloodlust. Surely one of the more shocking events in Angel Grove during the early days of the encounters, Spit Flower's presence and powers made for a terror-filled day throughout the city. This attack, ordered by Rita Repulsa, was rumored to have been in response to the World Peace Parade that was scheduled to take place the same day. Appearing first near the centralized bridge within the park, the Power Rangers were quick to respond to alerts and cries for help from frightened citizens. Upon their arrival, the Rangers fell prey to Spit Flower's terrifying biting blossoms before witnessing its massive growth. It was then, towering over the city, that Spit Flower drew in a huge breath, sucking up thousands of blossoms into its mouth only to be exhaled again as frightening flowers. Fortunately, the Rangers found a weak spot in Spit Flower's armor and, with the use of the Power Blaster, sent this bloom to its doom.

DESIGNATION
FRANKENSTEIN

Alias (Nickname)
Frankie
Known Abilities
**Neck-Bolt
Nunchucks,
Super Strength**

THE ANGEL GROVE YOUTH CENTER WAS BUSTLING WITH ACTIVITY FOR THE ANNUAL

Halloween Costume Party. But almost as soon as it had begun, costumed citizens noticed that something was awry; a man, only able to grunt and moan, arrived dressed as the iconic Frankenstein's Monster. After being swept onto the dance floor by a young woman, "Frankie" soon showed his true colors when he was shot in the head with a suction dart by none other than Farkas Bulkmeier and Eugene Skullovitch. This action seemed to bother the monster, who attacked Bulk and Skull and chased them from the Youth Center. Not much is clear about what transpired afterward. Eventually, there was an earthquake, which toppled several buildings set to be demolished anyway, followed by the appearance of Rita Repulsa herself, floating on a rock suspended over the city. Suddenly, Frankenstein appeared towering over the city and, after a battle with the Zords, was eventually defeated by the Rangers and their newly formed Dragonzord in Battle Mode. Once the city had calmed down, the Costume Party continued as planned. Apparently the "party crasher" had, indeed, been Rita's monster, sent to the event to pester partygoers for reasons unknown.

It should also be noted that this was the first of many Halloween parties that Alpha 5 would attend, pretending to be a young man in costume.

MUTITIS AND LOKAR THE TERRIBLE

Alias (Nickname)
n/a
Known Abilities
Mutitis: Toxic Foam,
Energy Blast
Lokar: Breath of
Doom

THE ARRIVAL OF LOKAR THE TERRIBLE AND HIS HIDEOUS CREATION, MUTITIS, WAS PRECEDED

by a vicious lightning storm and earthquake unlike anything Angel Grove had ever experienced. The Youth Center and most other businesses were evacuated due to the continued tremors as large storm clouds grew above the city, blocking out the sun and casting Angel Grove into darkness. According to Alpha 5's documents, Rita summoned Lokar the Terrible using an ancient magic spell. After witnessing his terrifying power many hundreds of years ago, she desired to utilize his heavy artillery once more. Prior to Lokar's arrival, the grotesque Mutitis appeared, already towering over the city. The Rangers arrived and, forming the Megazord, attempted to stop the monster's attack, only to have their Megazord knocked to the ground by Mutitis's ball and chain. Next, a flaming ball of fire descended from the moon and transformed into the ghastly floating face of Lokar, who cast down his fury upon the Rangers. Although the Dragonzord arrived and aided the Megazord in attacking the mutated Mutitis, both Zords fell victim to a violent energy blast from Mutitis's chest, followed by a stream of toxic foam, which brought down the mighty mechs and transported the

Rangers to the Island of Illusion. The Island of Illusion exists in an alternate dimension and floats, suspended among mysterious orange clouds. Not much is known about the Rangers' stay on the Island. Alpha's notes reveal very little. But it was apparent upon the return of the Rangers some time later that they had a score to settle. Quickly and without hesitation, the Megazord destroyed Mutitis. Lokar's defeat, however, called for a much mightier power. The Power Rangers summoned the magnificent Titanus and, forming the Ultrazord, fired upon Lokar's face in the sky, causing him to flee in fright. The clouds cleared, and the eye in the sky was no more.

DESIGNATION
ROCKSTAR

Alias (Nickname)
Rock Monster
Known Abilities
Projectile
Clinging
Body-Rocks

ONE OF THE MOST SHORT-LIVED CREATURE CREATIONS TO HAVE PLAGUED THE

Power Rangers, Rockstar entered the scene just as an encounter with Scorpina was reaching its climax. Leading up to the appearance of the boulder-faced bully, the Power Rangers had gotten themselves into a curious situation involving a young man, the beach, and a legendary and dangerous item known as the Mirror of Destruction. The battle had moved to a nearby beach club and there, Scorpina summoned Rockstar. The villainous creature made his debut by nearly drowning the Black and Yellow Rangers utilizing clinging body-rocks that launched from the creature's body. While his ability was dangerous, Rockstar soon met his end when the mysterious Mirror of Destruction was turned against him. The only other note regarding this encounter within Alpha 5's data is that the Mirror of Destruction was also destroyed at the end of the Megazord's sword.

DESIGNATION
SAMURAI FAN MAN

YEAR	ORIGIN	TYPE

Alias (Nickname)

n/a

Known Abilities

Magic Trap-Urn, Super Fan, Throwing Headdress Needles, Rake

THE MORNING OF THE SAMURAI FAN MAN'S ATTACK ON ANGEL GROVE WAS PRECEDED BY A

torrential downpour that ravaged the city from morning to midday. It was at this point that the Samurai Fan Man, sent by Rita to capture the Rangers in his enchanted urn, appeared in Angel Grove Park. Witnesses who encountered the Fan Man's initial touchdown were able to accurately describe the monster, but they soon fled the park for the sake of their lives. Shortly after this initial appearance, the Pink Ranger was captured in the Fan Man's urn by a cyclone-like force. The other Rangers were quick to arrive at the scene and battled valiantly against their newest foe. After nearly being launched into another dimension by the Fan Man's magical winds, the Power Rangers and their Zords faced off against a now-gigantic Fan Man and Goldar. With the arrival of the Dragonzord, the Pink Ranger was successfully freed. After a bold proclamation from the Fan Man stating that he would "knock [the Rangers] into the next galaxy," the villain was proved wrong with the arrival of Titanus and the formation of the Ultrazord. Needless to say, the only one knocked into the next galaxy that day was the Samurai Fan Man.

75

DESIGNATION

BABE RUTHLESS

YEAR	ORIGIN	TYPE

Alias (Nickname)
Baseball Monster
Known Abilities
Babe Ruthless:
Curve Ball Blast,
Horn Mist
Weaveworm:
Binding Cocoon

A PEACEFUL DAY AT THE BEACH TURNED GRIM UPON THE ARRIVAL OF NOT ONE BUT TWO

monsters escorted by Scorpina, Goldar, and a band of bumbling Putties. The Weaveworm, apparently a pet belonging to Scorpina, was the first of the two monsters to be brought into the fold. After appearing on the beach and being confronted by the Power Rangers, Scorpina revealed her slippery friend, who released a sudden and swift stream of translucent silk. This silk wrapped the Rangers in an unbreakable red cocoon that was then pushed over the cliffs and into the waves by the ever-eager Putties. Some time passed before the Rangers combined their Blade Blasters and burst forth from the cocoon. Soon after, the fight moved to a nearby industrial complex where the Rangers and their Zords faced down a goliath Scorpina, Goldar, and their second new encounter of the day, Babe Ruthless.

WEAVEWORM

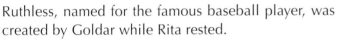

Ruthless, named for the famous baseball player, was created by Goldar while Rita rested.

After attempting to utilize a presumably poisonous mist, the barbaric batter produced a giant red ball, which he lobbed at the Tyrannosaurus Zord. With a swift swing of its tail, the Zord deflected one of Ruthless's attacks, causing him to charge and inevitably be brought down by a forceful blow through the chest by the Dragonzord's drill. Fearing defeat, Scorpina used an unknown source of magic to grow her Weaveworm and, once again, used its silk to bind the Megazord. This binding lasted only a moment. Soon, the Dragonzord returned and cut open the cocoon, freeing the Megazord and forming the Mega Dragonzord, a powerful combination of the two Zords, which made quick work of squashing the bothersome bug.

FANG

YEAR	ORIGIN	TYPE
①	☾	☺

Alias (Nickname)
Buck-Toothed Bully

Known Abilities
Razor-Sharp Claws,
Hidden Wrist
Blades, Head Beam

THE CREATURE KNOWN AS FANG, WHILE DANGEROUS IN HIS ACTIONS, SEEMED TO

cause more problems for his creators than he did for the Power Rangers. First witnessed running through the woods alone, the fishy fiend was heard chanting, "Destroy! Destroy!" over and over again in a high-pitched, squeaky voice. Later, appearing on the beach, Fang seemed furious at Squatt and Baboo, who had been spotted earlier in the day devouring several oversize eggs they'd stumbled upon in the sand. While it was assumed that these eggs were Fang's children, they were, in fact, only his lunch. One witness who maintained a fair distance reported hearing Fang "crying and threatening the two other aliens" as he howled on and on about how they'd eaten his "Goony-Bird eggs." Rita and Goldar eventually had to intervene to get Fang back on track. According to data, Rita and her minions convinced Fang that it was actually the Power Rangers who had eaten his eggs, thus leading to his ensuing rampage. Although vicious, Fang failed in his attempted destruction of the Angel Grove Dam. The Ultrazord, a masterful combination of the Mega Dragonzord and the legendary Titanus Zord, delivered the final blow, ending Fang's brief yet frightening encounter. Fang perished that day with an empty stomach.

DESIGNATION
CYCLOPS

YEAR	ORIGIN	TYPE

Alias (Nickname)
n/a
Known Abilities
Shape-Shifting,
Optical Energy
Blasts

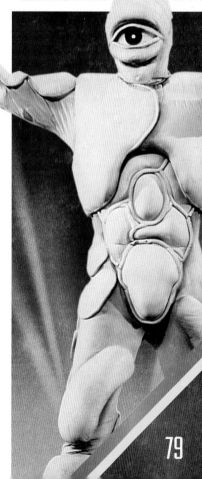

THE SAGA OF THE CYCLOPS IS A CONFUSING OCCURRENCE THAT

would appear to be the stuff of legend if not backed up by Alpha 5's data. The appearance of Rita's shape-shifting myth-monster coincides with another of Rita's plans to gain access to the power of the Green Ranger. According to transcripts, Rita had gained access to a special form of wax available only in the Gamma-Tri system that, once touched, retains an individual's personal energy. It was with a candle constructed from this wax that Rita planned on stealing the power of the Green Ranger once and for all.

After kidnapping the Green Ranger and locking him in one of her dimensional prisons, Rita sent the shape-shifting Cyclops to attack Angel Grove disguised as the Dragonzord. Similar to the real Dragonzord, the Cyclops imposter rose from the murky depths and destroyed several buildings throughout the seaside industrial district. No casualties were reported at the site, though property damage was extensive. Just as the fake Dragonzord touched down in the city, the remaining Rangers arrived with their trusty Megazord and were able to subdue the monster. At that point, the Green Ranger had already escaped Rita's clutches and arrived with the one true Dragonzord.

Continued on the following page

With a furious slash of its tail, the Dragonzord struck its evil counterpart, causing the Cyclops to revert to its true form. Armored, pale, and grotesque, the Cyclops had temporarily lost its ability to retain the Dragonzord form. The citizens stood in shock and awe at the magnificent transformation and retreat. Quickly, the Cyclops changed form once more, this time appearing as the Megazord. After several exhausting blows from the Dragonzord, the Cyclops reverted to its own form, firing a powerful optic blast before changing again, briefly, into the Tyrannosaurus Zord. Eventually, with the arrival of the Megazord and Titanus, the powerful Ultrazord was formed and fired a blast, ending the Cyclops's confusing yet brief existence.

HATCHASAURUS AND CARDIATRON

YEAR	ORIGIN	TYPE

Alias (Nickname)
Birdbrain
Known Abilities
Chest Spikes,
Laser Beam

THE GRUESOME TWOSOME KNOWN AS HATCHASAURUS AND CARDIATRON ARE A PARTICULARLY FASCINATING

combination of beings that operate in a strange, symbiotic relationship. Hatchasaurus, a frightful bird-like creature, rose from the ground near the Angel Grove Power Plant. Deep within this winged creature lies an intelligent, tentacle-clad organism known as Cardiatron. Cardiatron acts as the commander of Hatchasaurus and, upon Hatch's defeat, was able to rebuild his host and even endow it with greater power.

First destroyed in a combined effort by the Zords and the Dragonzord, Hatchasaurus was quick to return. Rebuilt piece by piece, he rose from an earthquake that split the ground near the mountains. It was during Hatchasaurus's second life that Cardiatron was able to take down the Megazord, at one point lifting it and throwing it through the air. Once again, the Megazord didn't stay down for long and succeeded in engulfing its foe in a brilliant firestorm. However, the Rangers soon learned that destroying Hatchasaurus might not be possible before destroying the true threat within—Cardiatron. The Red Ranger launched himself from the head of the Megazord into the jaws of Hatchasaurus.

After several moments Red emerged, grappling with the heart-like Cardiatron. Quickly, Red dispatched the hideous creature with the help of the Ultrazord. Hatchasaurus met its end moments later.

DESIGNATION
POLLUTICORN

Alias (Nickname)
Smog Breath
Known Abilities
Horn Blast,
Toxic Winds,
Near Invincibility

SENT DOWN BY RITA TO COVER THE PLANET IN POLLUTION, THE APPROPRIATELY NAMED

Polluticorn derives its poisonous power from the horn perched atop its head. The attack by Polluticorn took place on the same day that a clean-up-the-park initiative had been organized by a group of Angel Grove high-school students. The horse-like beast set about attacking the park and drawing out the Rangers quickly and efficiently. While the initial confrontation was brief, the Rangers and Polluticorn would come to blows later at the Angel Grove Recycling Plant. There, the unpleasant unicorn would be joined by Goldar and Scorpina. Polluticorn fought intensely against the Red Ranger while Goldar and Scorpina kept the others busy. It seemed as though Polluticorn was not expecting a one-on-one fight. The Red Ranger summoned his Dragon Shield and made quick work of severing the monster's power-giving horn from its head. In an effort to save the creature, Rita cast down her staff, making the Polluticorn grow. Unaffected, the Megazord withdrew the ever-faithful Power Sword and struck down the hazardous-waste monster.

ALTHOUGH RITA'S FIRST SHAPE-SHIFTING MONSTER (CYCLOPS) HAD FAILED,

she decided to give another changeling a try. Twin Man and a band of Putties were sent to Earth, led by the forever feisty Scorpina, to mimic the Power Rangers and turn the public against them. The ruse worked for a brief time. A little after noon, downtown Angel Grove reportedly erupted in a frenzy as pedestrians were violently attacked by the imposter Power Rangers. With no noticeable difference in uniform or weaponry, victims of this unprovoked attack truly believed that the Rangers had turned and joined the forces of evil that had for so long plagued their coastal city. Businesses, schools, and restaurants all locked down as hopeless residents braced for further attacks. Fortunately, they did not have to wait long. The true Power Rangers soon arrived and revealed the imposters to be nothing more than Putties and their leader, Twin Man, and no more attacks erupted. Once revealed, Twin Man attempted to attack the Rangers with his whip and magical mirror vision. The doppelganger briefly incapacitated the Rangers before being destroyed by the combined power of the Power Blaster. Angel Grove's local news was on-site to confirm that the imposters had been destroyed and the city was safe once more.

OCTOPLANT

Alias (Nickname)
Bulb Brain

Known Abilities
Optical Energy
Blasts, Tentacles

THE OCTOPLANT, WHOSE SEEDS WERE SOWN BY SQUATT IN ANGEL GROVE PARK, WAS SENT

to Angel Grove to grow and grow until its tentacles encircled the entire globe. Thankfully, the Power Rangers prevented this from ever happening, but the road to stopping the Octoplant was certainly not without its obstacles.

Sent by Rita to plant the Octoplant seeds, Squatt was first sighted in the park by Bulk and Skull, who had an unfortunate run-in with the blue creature. Although they denied screaming and running away, another witness said that the two were seen jumping into a nearby Porta Potty to hide while Squatt went about digging and planting his seeds. Prior to the vile vegetation rising from the ground, a series of overgrown and vicious tentacles attacked and bound the Red Ranger, who was, fortunately, saved moments later by his fellow Rangers. These seeds, protected by an energy field resembling pink lightning, eventually blossomed and gave birth to the Octoplant. After Rita made the Octoplant grow, the beautiful monstrosity soon found itself distracted by its own reflection in a nearby building. The Megazord made quick work of whacking the weed and making the city safe once again.

DESIGNATION

GOO FISH

YEAR	ORIGIN	TYPE
I	☾	💧

Alias (Nickname)
Overgrown Herring
Known Abilities
Immobilizing
Venom, Staff,
Exploding Starfish

AN UNSIGHTLY, SLIPPERY SEA CREATURE, GOO FISH WAS THE FIRST OF MANY FIENDISH

fish beasts to plague the Power Rangers and the city they were sworn to protect. Rita unleashed her newest creation during a sunny day on Angel Grove Beach as many residents enjoyed the welcoming waves. From these waves, Goo Fish emerged and was immediately met by the Pink and Blue Rangers, who did their best to handle the creature on their own. Alpha 5's data indicates that the Blue Ranger, frightened of fish, took refuge behind his pink partner. Upon the arrival of the remaining Rangers, Goo Fish retreated into the water only to emerge hours later with a platoon of Putties to pester the Rangers once more. In their final encounter, Goo Fish succeeded in subduing three of his enemies (Red, Black, and Yellow Rangers) with his venom while launching an exploding starfish at the Pink Ranger. Thus, it was left to the Blue Ranger to battle the slimy sea monster. With a cunning play of jumping about and confusing Goo Fish, the Blue Ranger caused his enemy to be the victim of his own venom. Seeing the declining situation, Rita cast down her staff, making Goo Fish visible to the entire city. After a thrilling battle, the Megazord succeeded in filleting the furious fish.

DESIGNATION
GOATAN

Alias (Nickname)
The Storm-Bringer
Known Abilities
Bow and Arrows,
Hockey Stick,
Weather
Manipulation

THE ULTIMATE PRIZE FOR WINNING THE ANNUAL ANGEL GROVE ODDBALL GAMES

is the Noble Lion Trophy. This coveted award was to be the next target of Rita's dark magic. After the trophy was stolen by local troublemakers Bulk and Skull, Rita transformed the prized statue into the terrible chimera monster, Goatan. The beast promptly threw the two thieves into the lake, according to witnesses at the scene. Bulk and Skull debate the veracity of these claims, though Alpha 5's data suggests them to be true.

Soon after the appearance of Goatan at the lake, a terrible storm rolled in and surrounded the city: A tornado watch was put into effect by local meteorologists. The Rangers were transported to the mountains to battle Goatan, who utilized both his weather-manipulating abilities and his strong bow. Eventually, after being grown by Rita, Goatan faced the Megazord and, ultimately, fell before its might. The skies cleared above Angel Grove, and Goatan was never seen again.

FIGHTING FLEA

YEAR	ORIGIN	TYPE

Alias (Nickname)
Bug Breath
Known Abilities
Contagious Bite,
Projectile Darts,
Laser Antennae

ON THE SAME DAY THAT THE POPULAR ANGEL GROVE YOUTH CENTER SADLY ANNOUNCED ITS

closing, Rita ordered Finster to craft a creation that would bring an end to the Power Rangers. The monster, Fighting Flea, first appeared in the park. Unlike monsters of the past who loudly made their appearance known, Rita shrank the monster to the size of a small pest. Thus, the Fighting Flea infiltrated Angel Grove on the back of a small, lost pup that had been found by Angel Grove high-school students. A passerby in the park reported that a party of Putties arrived around midday and attacked the students before running away, covered in a writhing cloud of red insects—presumably the Putties had come into contact with the dog and contracted the Fighting Flea's army of insects. The Flea later appeared in full form to none other than Bulk and Skull. Allegedly, the two ran away, avoiding any further conflict. The Flea, itching for a fight, appeared again at the local junk yard where he finally met the Power Rangers. After a frantic fight against the Megazord, the bug was exterminated in battle. The lost dog mentioned earlier was eventually returned to its owner, a wealthy Angel Grove socialite, who rewarded the Youth Center with a healthy sum, thus halting its closure.

DESIGNATION
JELLYFISH WARRIOR

YEAR | ORIGIN | TYPE

Alias (Nickname)
Slime
Known Abilities
Toxic Spray,
Umbrella Shield,
Tentacle Arm

WIELDING A POWERFUL TOXIC ACID, THE JELLYFISH WARRIOR TESTED THE VERY LIMITS

of the Power Rangers' protective armor. This stinging scalawag boasts an obnoxious array of abilities that gave Angel Grove a reasonable fright. Ms. Appleby, a kindly educator at Angel Grove High, had tasked her students with filling a time capsule. The time capsule was stolen by Rita's minions, Squatt and Baboo, soon after it arrived in the park. Once the capsule was stolen, the Jellyfish Warrior appeared and was instantaneously met by the Power Rangers. But after a quick spray of its toxic acid, the Rangers retreated to the Command Center, where Alpha 5 reinforced their suits with a powerful protectant. The Jellyfish Warrior was once again met by the Power Rangers at the Botanical Gardens. Without notice, the Jellyfish Warrior whipped out an umbrella-like shield that, upon turning, transported the Rangers to another dimension. Moments later, the Rangers would return thanks to the Black Ranger's success in striking the Jellyfish Warrior with his axe. Calling upon their Zords, the Power Rangers triumphed in jamming the giant Jellyfish with a swift swing of the Power Sword.

MANTIS

Alias (Nickname)
Monster Bug
Known Abilities
Master of Praying
Mantis Kung Fu,
Teleportation

IT IS SURELY NO COINCIDENCE THAT THE CREATION OF THE MANTIS MONSTER

coincided with the arrival of the esteemed Master Lee, a master of the Praying Mantis Kung Fu style, to Angel Grove. While Master Lee never had an opportunity to show the indignant insect a thing or two, the Yellow Ranger surely would have received his praise after her expertly executed battle against the kung fu creepy-crawly. According to Alpha 5, the Yellow Ranger had been practicing the Mantis form of kung fu for many months before the battle and was, thus, able to perfectly counter her foe.

After an initial standoff in the woods near the park, the Mantis and the Yellow Ranger faced each other for the final time in the old quarry. When the other Rangers arrived, Rita sent Putties to hold them back from the duel of the day. The Mantis, fearing defeat at the hands of his foe, called upon the Putties to attack. But the Yellow Ranger was quick, delivering a brutal blow with her daggers across the insect's stomach. Despite being grown to a monstrous size by Rita, the Mantis was cut down by a single swipe of the Megazord's Power Sword.

DRAMOLE

YEAR	ORIGIN	TYPE

Alias (Nickname)
Disgusting Rat

Known Abilities
Teleportation, Hypnotizing Gas, Enhanced Burrowing Ability

PHOTO FROM LATER ENCOUNTER

A SMALL YET CRUCIAL PAWN IN ONE OF RITA'S PLANS FOR WORLD DOMINATION, DRAMOLE

is often overlooked among the Power Rangers' most aggressive adversaries. The events surrounding the arrival of Dramole are far more outstanding than the creature itself. Essentially, Rita utilized Dramole, with his hypnotic and teleporting abilities, in the abduction of countless citizens of Angel Grove who had gathered at the Youth Center for a Parents' Day celebration. The rat creature tunneled beneath the building and caused a violent tremor before unleashing his hypnotic gas that successfully transported the parents to another dimension. There, Rita kept the citizens captive, holding them for ransom. Alpha's data revealed little about the particular event, but it is rumored that Rita was somehow trying to obtain the power of the Green Ranger.

Ultimately, the events of the day led to a brief and unexpected reappearance of the Green Ranger. With the help of his fellow Rangers, the Green Ranger defeated Dramole, thus releasing the abducted parents from captivity. While Rita failed once again, it cannot be denied that Dramole's role in the events of the day made the majority of Rita's plan work.

DESIGNATION
GRUMBLE BEE

Alias (Nickname)
Pollen Breath
Known Abilities
Lethal Venom,
Poisonous Stingers,
Harmful Ultrasonic
Tones

BEES ARE OFTEN SADDLED WITH A POOR REPUTATION DUE TO THEIR PAINFUL STINGERS.

However, bees are essential in the cross-pollination of many plants on Earth and are absolutely essential to human beings' survival as a species. So, while many may fear bees and their sting, it's best to leave them alone and let them go about their jobs.

The same kindness cannot and should not be extended to the moon monster known as Grumble Bee. This oversize pollinator was outfitted with a lethal and corrosive venom, projectile poisonous stingers, and a harmful ultrasonic emission. Similar to the Jellyfish Warrior, Grumble Bee's venom was able to nearly eat through the protective armor of the Blue Ranger. Surviving the encounter, the Rangers returned with a special device created by Alpha 5 that coated the bee in a layer of binding foam. This, sadly, only lasted for moments before Rita intervened and made the already irksome insect giant. The Megazord, enduring Grumble's stingers and ultrasonic blast, was able to squash the bug for good, thus alleviating Angel Grove of the unwanted pest.

DESIGNATION

TWO-HEADED PARROT

YEAR	ORIGIN	TYPE

Alias (Nickname)
Birdbrain
Known Abilities
Dual Optic Blast,
Projectile Feather
Darts, Nostril
Missiles

WITH TWICE AS MANY BRAINS AS RITA'S PREVIOUS MONSTERS, THE TWO-HEADED PARROT

might have succeeded if it hadn't ended up fighting with itself over a favorite fruit. Commissioned by Rita for its soaring intelligence, the Two-Headed Parrot was seemingly one of Finster's better creations. With a frightful dual optic blast and fearsomely fast projectile feathers, this double dodo should have been able to defeat the Power Rangers with ease. However, with the help of the ever-intelligent Blue Ranger, the Rangers discovered the Two-Headed Parrot's weakness—the pamango fruit. Because the fruit was available in Angel Grove Park, the Rangers quickly set out to find the perfect distracting dinner before learning that the Putties had picked them all and fled with arms full. Somehow, after surviving the Two-Headed Parrot's dual optic blast, the Green Ranger arrived right on time with pamango in hand. Tossing the flavorful fruit into the hands of the plumed pair created an instant argument between the two heads about who deserved the delectable fruit more. Unfortunately, this distraction left the Parrot open to attack. Despite Rita's giant spell, the Dragonzord and Megazord were able to send the Two-Headed Parrot home to roost.

PECKSTER

YEAR	ORIGIN	TYPE

Alias (Nickname)
Seed Breath
Known Abilities
Windstorm Wings,
Projectile Beak Bolts

SENT WITH THE MISSION TO DESTROY EVERY BUILDING IN ANGEL GROVE, THE APTLY NAMED

Peckster was set up for failure from the very beginning. An emergency broadcast rang through all of Angel Grove, interrupting regularly scheduled programs, to bring a frightful message: "This wretched woodpecker wreaks havoc upon our fair city. Buildings fall with just a few pecks from its horrendous beak into huge piles of rubble." The Black Ranger, wielding his mighty Power Axe, was the first to arrive on the scene. Peckster dealt a violent blow with its beak, which destroyed the axe and led the Black Ranger to retreat. Later, spotted flying over the industrial area near the outskirts of the city, Peckster was met by the other Power Rangers, who succeeded in holding off the half-baked bird while the Black Ranger arrived with an ingenious scheme. Holding a bouquet of black balloons, the Black Ranger taunted Peckster. The bird, in turn, popped all the balloons before getting its beak lodged in the final one—which was not a balloon at all, but a decoy ball. The Rangers fired on Peckster with their Blade Blasters just as Rita decided to intervene. While the battle with the Megazord was memorable, Peckster fell after only minutes due to a dramatic swipe of the Power Sword.

DESIGNATION
PUMPKIN RAPPER

Alias (Nickname)
Squash Brain
Known Abilities
Electrified Vines,
Mega-Pumpkin
Shock, Hypnotic
Raps

ARGUABLY THE MOST UNEXPECTED OF RITA'S CREATIONS, THE PUMPKIN RAPPER

turned out to be one of the Power Rangers' most frightful foes. Planted in the park by Squatt and Baboo, rotten pumpkin seeds grew into a perilous patch of pumpkins that ultimately led to the rise of the Pumpkin Rapper. As reported by an eyewitness, the pumpkins in the park began to shake back and forth as if attempting to free themselves from their vines. The Rangers were alerted to this particular patch by the intelligence of Zordon, and arrived soon after. Immediately upon inspecting the strange plants, the Rangers (excluding Pink) nearly met their end when the putrid plants attached themselves to their helmets. Unable to breathe or see, the Power Rangers panicked before being saved by the Pink Ranger, who smartly cut the pumpkins from the Rangers' heads. The Pumpkin Rapper, wielding his hypnotic raps, did rise soon after. Luckily, with the sudden arrival of the Green Ranger, the vile vegetable's vines were cut and the combined might of the Power Blaster sent the ridiculous rapper to an early grave.

DESIGNATION

SOCCADILLO

Alias (Nickname)
Rodent
Known Abilities
Unbreakable Armor, Wrist Blast, Optic Blast

WHEN FINSTER CAME INTO POSSESSION OF A SOCCADILLO BALL—A RARE ITEM THAT, WHEN

energized, releases the monster within—it was Rita's immediate decision to use the extraterrestrial creature against the Power Rangers. The Soccadillo ball first appeared in the park while a group of local Angel Grove High students were playing soccer. Eyewitnesses say that a group of Putties entered into a strange game of soccer with the students until the "strange gray ball" apparently "began floating in the air and trying to strike the players." It was at this point that the witnesses fled in fright. The Soccadillo, no longer in ball form, appeared later beneath the bluffs by the ocean at the edge of Angel Grove. There, it was met by the Power Rangers, who utilized a tower formation to fire their Blade Blasters in unison. The Soccadillo, quickly reverting to its spherical form, deflected the attack. Putties soon appeared and, again, kicked the Soccadillo ball at the Rangers before the fortuitous arrival of the Green Ranger, who quickly knocked the Soccadillo out of its ball form. Fearing its defeat by the Rangers' various weapons, Rita made the Soccadillo grow. Despite the Soccadillo claiming to be "invincible," the Megazord and Dragonzord defeated the bowling ball–like brawler with a finishing blow of the Power Sword.

DESIGNATION

SLIPPERY SHARK

YEAR	ORIGIN	TYPE
1	🌙	💧

Alias (Nickname)
Fish Face

Known Abilities
Magical Fish Boomerang, Mastery of Spells, Teleportation

SLIPPERY SHARK WAS FAR MORE DANGEROUS THAN HIS EARTHBOUND LIKENESS.

While most sharks in our seas are relatively docile toward humans, Rita's creation was brought to life to be the opposite. Weaving around beneath the soil, the Slippery Shark is a cunning and elusive extraterrestrial invader with simple trickery as its most powerful weapon. Wielding a fish-like boomerang that held spell-casting powers, this aquatic adversary utilized its powers to turn the Green Ranger and the Red Ranger against each other. The event happened in the park, where the Shark wove beneath the grass. The Red and Green Rangers initially fought each other before overcoming their spell-cast competitiveness and netting the ground-bound predator. Using the boomerang to cut itself free, the Slippery Shark attempted to take on the Rangers with swift swats. However, the Black Ranger was quick on his feet and on the trigger, firing a blast from his axe, which caused the slippery scamp to emerge, smoking, from the earth. Growing suddenly with help from Rita's ever-intrusive staff, the Slippery Shark eventually floundered after a hearty battle against the Megazord.

DESIGNATION
LIZZINATOR

Alias (Nickname)
n/a
Known Abilities
Laser Eyes,
Super Stink Breath

WITH AN EXOSKELETON MADE OF SUPERMETAL FROM ANOTHER GALAXY, THE LIZZINATOR

could have been the monster to finally end the Power Rangers. This lizard creature made its explosive debut on the grounds of one of Angel Grove's shipping centers near the water, where it burst through a heavy cement wall and sent nearby citizens running for their lives.

Despite heroic efforts by the Red Ranger, the Lizzinator showed its true strength when it lifted a vehicle above its head and threw it at its newfound challenger before disappearing in a hazy purple cloud. Later, the fanged foe reappeared near a mining site in the mountains where it was met by the full force of the Rangers. After being grown and then defeated in a terrible tussle with the Megazord and Dragonzord, the Lizzinator exploded in a spectacular array of sparks. It was later revealed that the Lizzinator had actually been a clever cover-up for the attempted abduction of a young Angel Grovian who was found safe and sound by the city's protectors. It remains unknown why the specific child was taken, but some have speculated that the student may have been associated with the Power Rangers in some way or another.

DESIGNATION

RHINO BLASTER

YEAR	ORIGIN	TYPE

Alias (Nickname)
Quarterback
Known Abilities
Multidimensional
Mist, Horn Blast,
Sword

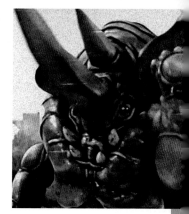

ALTHOUGH THE NAME SUGGESTS OTHERWISE, IT WOULD BE FAR MORE APPROPRIATE TO

refer to Rhino Blaster as a crude-looking quarterback than a rhinoceros.

Bored and frustrated from her multiple defeats, Rita decided to have some fun by sending her "football beast" to touch down in Angel Grove.

Rhino Blaster's first appearance was preceded by a Putty attack. According to several eyewitnesses, the Putties interrupted a friendly game of flag football between some students. The identities of the youths are unknown, but whatever the cause of the sudden interruption, it surely led to the follow-up encounter with the Power Rangers outside the city. It was there that the Rhino Blaster appeared with a ragtag team of Putties dressed in football jerseys who proceeded to face off against the hometown heroes in a game of football. Serving as the quarterback, the Rhino Blaster resorted to his multidimensional mist, which captured its victims in a strange tornado-like tunnel and transported them to a far-off place. Thanks to the astounding heroism of the Green Ranger, who knew to throw his Dragon Dagger into the multidimensional mist, the Rangers were rescued and Rhino Blaster was destroyed.

COMMANDER CRAYFISH AND THE MUTANT RANGERS

YEAR	ORIGIN	TYPE

Overgrown Seafood Platter

Known Abilities

Sword, Command of Mutant Rangers

SIMILAR TO THE PREVIOUS ENCOUNTER WITH THE LIZZINATOR, THE POWER RANGERS ONCE AGAIN

faced a gang of special Putties, this time under the banner of a cutthroat crustacean. Rita delved deep into her dark caverns on the moon to bring to light the Badges of Darkness. With these badges, Rita imparted powers upon a select group of Putties. These Putties, trained by Goldar himself, were morphed into the menacing Mutant Rangers and led into battle by Finster's newest creation, Commander Crayfish. The crusty controller of the replica Rangers proceeded to challenge the Power Rangers near the Angel Grove shoreline. There, the Rangers faced off against their dangerous doppelgangers until one fateful moment when both sides of the skirmish pulled Blade Blasters and fired on each other. The Rangers' blasters, forever faithful, overwhelmed the fakes. Commander Crayfish and the Mutant Rangers grew to fearful heights, but fell fast at the mechanical hands of the mighty Megazord.

DESIGNATION
OYSTERIZER

Alias (Nickname)
Oyster Soup
Known Abilities
Acid Gel, Optical
Energy Blast, Pearl
and Chain

WHILE MANY IMPORTANT DETAILS ARE MISSING IN ALPHA 5'S ACCOUNT OF THE

Oysterizer incident, eyewitness testimonies have been somewhat more revealing. The weather was fine and the skies were clear when Angel Grove citizens gathered at a local French restaurant. As laughter and joy spread through the air, so did something a bit more sinister. Suddenly, as if by magic, all persons inside of the restaurant were frozen, their skin turned a drab shade of gray. Sometime later, the Oysterizer rose from the depths of Angel Grove Lake, where it was met by both the Black and Green Rangers. After a quick spat involving the Oysterizer's projectile acidic gel, the creature was quickly kicked back into the water by the heroic efforts of the Black Ranger. It was at this time that the "spell" allegedly was broken at the French restaurant and the diners were freed from their frozen, statue-like state. Soon, a battle would break out on the beach between the Oysterizer, the Megazord, and the Dragonzord. Needless to say, the cunning clam was defeated, and the town was able to return to its evening entertainment.

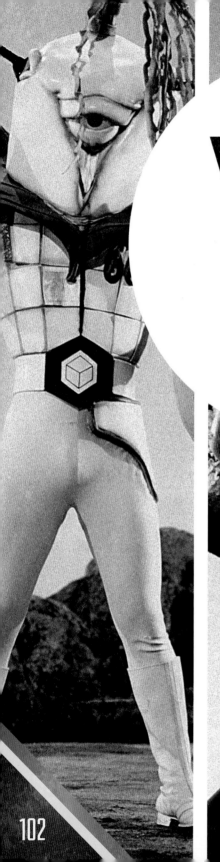

YEAR TWO

(1994–1995)

THE SECOND WAVE

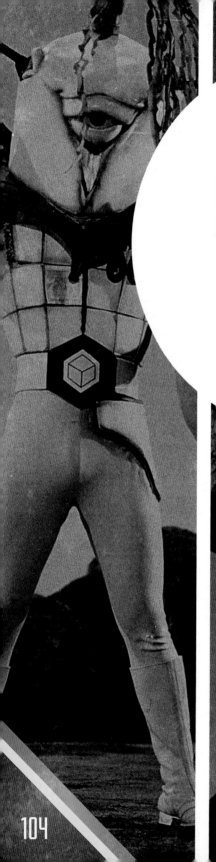
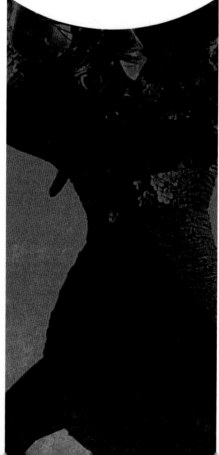

PART
ONE

A
NEW THREAT

THE FIRST SWITCH-UP
EMPEROR IN EMPRESS OUT

Rita Repulsa had awakened the world to barbaric brutes from faraway galaxies and evil extraterrestrials manufactured on our very own moon. Creatures crafted out of clay by the foul Finster and his magnificently malevolent Monster-Matic™ rained down on the city of Angel Grove, unexpected and awful in ways previously unknown to our world. Often preceded by patrols of Putties, these antagonistic aliens were turned into towering terrors taller than the highest buildings by Rita Repulsa's dark magic. Against these foes, the Power Rangers rose and fought the fiendish forces of the Empress of Evil. On the verge of victory, the protectors of our planet watched as a new dark force arrived from across the stars. Gone were the days of manufactured monsters. Lord Zedd had arrived and brought with him a new environment of evil that even Zordon could not have predicted. So began the nerve-racking reign of the true Emperor of Evil.

DESIGNATION

LORD ZEDD

Alias (Nickname)
Emperor of Evil,
Prince of Darkness

Known Abilities
Z-Staff,
Enhanced Vision,
Dark Magic

**ALPHA 5'S
MENACE
METER**

▶ Run. Please, run.

Take Cover.

Keep Away.

Mostly Harmless.

BY THE TIME LORD ZEDD ARRIVED ON THE SCENE, THE CITIZENS OF ANGEL GROVE THOUGHT THEY HAD SEEN EVERYTHING: BLABBERING MONSTERS MADE OF CLAY, AN OVEREATING PIG, A CREATURE COMPRISED

entirely of eyes, and a savage parrot with two heads. These were the flavors of the week. And though dangerous, they were absurd in appearance and often easily beaten by the Power Rangers. Zedd changed all of this. Rare photos taken of the moon by Angel Grove's quaint observatory paint a fearsome picture of the Power Rangers' most terrifying foe.

In order to properly explain Zedd's gruesome appearance, it is essential to delve into the self-proclaimed Emperor of Evil's past. While much of Zedd's history is based on legend and hearsay, the details presented are too stirring to omit. According to Alpha 5, Lord Zedd's current appearance originated many hundreds (if not thousands) of years ago in a distant place unknown to the people of Earth.

It was during this time that Zedd, already feared throughout the universe, attempted to take the coveted Zeo Crystal for himself. The Zeo Crystal is an ancient and extraordinarily powerful relic that currently remains hidden. Allegedly, Zedd believed that the strength of the crystal would bring all of his enemies to their knees. Unbeknownst to Lord Zedd, the Zeo Crystal bears magical defenses that protect it against forces of evil. According to legend, as Zedd took it in his hands, the protective powers instantly lashed out and tore the flesh from his body, nearly killing him in the process.

It was many years before Zedd

would emerge again to once more set out on his quest of galactic domination. In the days that followed, legend has it that he was ashamed of his weakened state and wore a cloak to cover his deformity.

What we do know for certain is no less astounding. Lord Zedd bears no flesh and is therefore covered in exposed crimson muscles protected by a shimmering steel exoskeleton of unknown origin. The exoskeleton comes complete with razor-sharp gauntlets, a skeletal chest piece, and a frightening steel mask, which all make for a disfigured and scarred visage. The mask is adorned with a dark ruby visor that shields the bare eyes beneath, a breathing apparatus that forms a horrific smile, and to top it all off, a headpiece on which protrudes a twelve-inch spire topped with a jagged "Z." Lastly, the exposed brain atop Zedd's head pulses with movement. When Zedd arrived at the Moon Palace, he wore no cloak to cover his being, thus giving the citizens of Earth a frightening view to behold.

APPEARANCE ASIDE, ZEDD'S TRUE THREAT IS NOT HIS EXTREMELY REPULSIVE VENEER.

After arriving at the Moon Palace, Zedd disposed of Rita Repulsa because of her continued failures in his service, taking it upon himself to defeat the Power Rangers once and for all. Rita's minions, Goldar in particular, quickly took to their new master and aided him in his far more meticulous endeavors. Gone were the days of Finster creating his own monsters. Zedd had powers beyond Rita's dreams. It is widely rumored and generally agreed that Lord Zedd had a strong grasp on dark magic, which he channeled through both his mighty staff and

CENTENNIAL RECHARGE
ZEDD'S BIG SLEEP

Every one hundred years, Lord Zedd enters into a deep sleep that is most definitely not to be disturbed. While the reason for this recharge is unknown, it can most likely be attributed to Zedd's constant attempts at conquest of the galaxy—during which he rarely rests. A special Rejuvenation Chamber lies deep within the Moon Palace, where tubes are connected to the vile villain, supplying him with further means of energy. Details about the time spent within this recharge are unknown.

his own body. When Zedd wished to attack the Power Rangers, he didn't require a design. The monsters under his control were made from real animals and assorted objects already on Earth—anything that Zedd imagined could be used as a weapon against his enemies. Many theorists and fanatics believe this to be a far more efficient process by which to create a creature of pure destruction.

WHILE RITA WOULD SEND DOWN HER STAFF IN ORDER TO MAKE MONSTERS GIGANTIC, ZEDD NO LONGER NEEDED TO PART WITH HIS OWN STAFF TO EXECUTE THE SAME POWER.

He would summon what some call a "growth bomb," toss it to the monster, and see the desired effects. In addition to his dark magic, Zedd also has enhanced vision, which allows him to see events transpiring on Earth or anywhere else in the galaxy without the use of a telescope or other such devices.

Although Lord Zedd presents himself as a violent and unpredictable foe, the Power Rangers have been smart enough and fortunate enough to foil his schemes time and time again.

PINK IN POWER

ZEDD'S ATTEMPT AT ACQUIRING A NEW QUEEN

During his reign within the Moon Palace, Lord Zedd sought a queen from Earth. That queen, if Zedd had had his way, would have been the Pink Ranger. Far before his wedding to Rita Repulsa, Zedd sent several of his minions to Earth in order to convince the powerful Pink Ranger that she would make a proper wife for the Emperor of Evil. The Pink Ranger, obviously strong-willed and against any kind of evil, fooled Zedd's minions and escaped capture.

DESIGNATION
SERPENTERA

Alias (Nickname)
Zedd's Zord
Known Abilities
Space Flight,
Immovable Weight,
Weaponry Unknown

**ALPHA 5'S
MENACE
METER**

Run. Please, run.

▶ Take Cover.

Keep Away.

Mostly Harmless.

SERPENTERA, THE ONE AND ONLY ZORD IN THIS COLLECTION OF ENCOUNTERS TO MERIT ITS OWN PROFILE, WAS CERTAINLY THE MOST FRIGHTFUL FIGURE TO EVER APPEAR IN ANGEL GROVE.

The first detail of note was Serpentera's incredible size, roughly that of two to three buildings stacked on top of one another. The Megazord, Dragonzord, and even Goldar's Zord, Cyclopsis, paled in comparison to the magnitude of Serpentera. Its sheer size made it a prominent threat whenever it was brought to Earth. However, when Zedd's Zord did arrive in Angel Grove, it merely landed and stood there. While this action was largely considered by the people of Angel Grove to be a means of intimidation, the real explanation for this behavior was far simpler. When building the biggest Zord the galaxy had ever seen, Zedd had forgotten to develop an energy source to sustain it. Therefore, Serpentera's power source was completely burned out by the time it landed on Earth. The people of Earth were therefore thankful for Zedd's gross oversight. According to Alpha 5's data, Serpentera did succeed in disassembling the Thunder Megazord once, but was unable to finish the job due to the arrival of the impenetrable Tor, who hid the Megazord beneath its armor. Of course,

Zedd later attempted to steal a significant power source in order to properly utilize Serpentera during the Bookala encounter. He emerged unsuccessful.

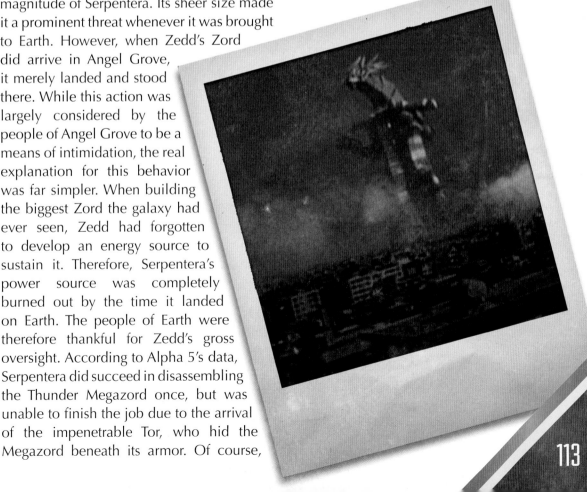

PART TWO

EVIL SPACE ALIENS: PRODUCED ON OUR PLANET

PIRANTISHEAD

Alias (Nickname)
Overgrown Guppy
Known Abilities
Freeze Ray,
Nunchucks,
Fish Flute

THE ARRIVAL OF ZEDD'S FIRST CREATION, A FEROCIOUS FISH KNOWN AS PIRANTISHEAD,

ushered in a new level of danger for both Angel Grove and the Power Rangers. Casting down a bolt of lightning from his dreaded Z-Staff, the new Lord of the Moon transformed an innocent piranha in the Rampoon River into a terrible and incredible creature. Pirantishead terrified the ever-present Bulk and Skull during the Fifth Annual Children's Hospital Charity Motor Marathon by making their four-wheelers run backward and out of control. But this creature also undertook more sinister assignments. Standing atop one of the many buildings in Angel Grove, Pirantishead utilized his multipurpose nunchucks to send a ruinous ray that destroyed a nearby building. Immediately after this malicious move, the foul fish froze the arriving Zords, leaving only the Tyrannosaurus, which he then took control of and ordered to destroy the city. Fortunately for the fair citizens of Angel Grove, the Power Rangers, while momentarily without Zords, rallied once more, arriving with new Zords and destroying Pirantishead with much fanfare. While Zedd had meant to make a point of his arrival, he only succeeded in providing further proof that the Power Rangers were here to protect.

DESIGNATION
PRIMATOR

Alias (Nickname)
Bone-Headed
Baboon
Known Abilities
Shape-Shifting,
Iron Staff

CREATED FROM A DISCARDED GORILLA SUIT, PRIMATOR APPEARED TO BE THE

hybrid of an ape and a blue-faced baboon. While he was less than formidable in hand-to-hand combat, his true strength lay in his deceiving nature. Primator was a shape shifter with the ability to mimic his enemies, causing confusion in confrontations. When this banana-breathed beast wasn't bounding about, beating his chest, and cackling wildly, he was turning friends into enemies. Eyewitnesses reported seeing Primator successfully mimic the appearance of the Rangers. If it hadn't been for a simple mirror that revealed Primator's true form, the Rangers might have been defeated. Luckily, this was not the case. After growing to an enormous size thanks to one of Lord Zedd's growth bombs, Primator's monkey business was quickly shut down by the Mega Thunderzord, a new Megazord composed of the Thunderzords forged from the remains of the nearly destroyed Dinozords.

DESIGNATION

SALIGUANA

Alias (Nickname)
Lizard Breath
Known Abilities
Fire Breath

WITH A LONG SPIKED TAIL AND ROWS OF SHARP TEETH, THIS REVOLTING REPTILE PROVED

to be a competent yet overly confident foe. While Saliguana's appearance would normally put any normal individual on edge, the Power Rangers are definitely not normal. Faced with the piercing red eyes of this scaled savage, the heroes of Angel Grove once again delivered on their promise to protect its citizens.

Saliguana's ability to breathe fire, along with an extremely strong prehensile tongue, made for a fearsome threat. However, the creature's fire was literally extinguished and his tongue severed during a battle with the Mega Thunderzord that ultimately led to his demise. One witness believed that Saliguana was related to an iguana owned by Angel Grove High School's very own Ms. Appleby. Eugene Skullovitch claimed that Appleby's iguana was absent during the events of Saliguana's attack, but upon the villain's defeat, the lizard was once again discovered in her classroom. However, Alpha 5's notes on the incident failed to corroborate Skull's statement.

BLOOM OF DOOM

YEAR	ORIGIN	TYPE
2		

Alias (Nickname)
Flower Brain
Known Abilities
Poisonous Pollen,
Vine Tentacles

LOVELY, LEAFY, AND LETHAL—THESE THREE WORDS DESCRIBE ZEDD'S FOURTH

Earth-threatening creation. The Bloom of Doom, while disruptive and dangerous, didn't pose much of a physical threat to the Power Rangers. Lord Zedd sent a Putty disguised in a trench coat to Earth to deliver a deceptive potion to the Pink Ranger that instilled in her feelings of disgust and anger toward her fellow Rangers. Using this influence to his advantage, Lord Zedd created the Bloom of Doom in Angel Grove Park, whereupon it was met by the Power Rangers. Arguing ensued between the Pink Ranger and her associates, yet the spell was eventually overcome in the face of dire circumstances. The Bloom of Doom, according to Alpha 5's data, transported herself and the Pink Ranger to a "little garden," which existed in an interdimensional warp. It was there that the Pink Ranger, having overcome Zedd's potent potion, fought the frightful flower and, with the help of the Yellow Ranger, destroyed her.

DESIGNATION
ROBOGOAT

YEAR	ORIGIN	TYPE
2		

Alias (Nickname)
Goat Cheese
Known Abilities
Rod of Destruction,
Sword of Power,
Energy Projection

THE ROBOGOAT WAS A SINISTER CYBORG SUPPOSEDLY CREATED BY ZEDD, UTILIZING A

popular book on mythology. One of its most notable achievements was the brief wielding and usage of the Sword of Power, an ancient weapon potentially similar to the Green Ranger's Sword of Darkness. Though this information cannot be verified, the power of the sword cannot be questioned; the very fact that Zedd wished to possess the sword is proof enough of its power. After Goldar had somehow successfully stolen the sword from the Rangers, it fell into the claws of the Robogoat, who cast powerful beams of lightning from the sword toward its combatants. Thrusting the sword into the rough terrain beneath its feet, the ghastly goat opened up a chasm into which the Rangers fell—except for the Red Ranger! In a dramatic duel, metal met metal as the Red Ranger challenged the Sword of Power with his own Power Sword. After the Red Ranger knocked the weapon from the Robogoat's clinging claws, the Sword of Power vanished and, according to Alpha 5, returned to the Command Center, where it would remain safe. The Rangers, released from orbs emanating from the cyborg's chest, rallied and defeated the then-overgrown goat after a brief bout of lightning and a swing of the Thunder Megazord's sword.

OCTOPHANTOM

Alias (Nickname)
Creep
Known Abilities
Magic Jar,
Optical Energy
Blast, Staff,
Electric Binds

THE OCTOPHANTOM SEEMED FASCINATED AND INCREDIBLY ENGROSSED WITH ITS OWN

image. The hybrid horror, a combination of octopus and elephant, put the Rangers through the wringer for several hours during the encounter. Unfortunately, while the skirmishes were stimulating, the Octophantom's continued obsession with its appearance made for a far more absorbing account. After arriving in Angel Grove Park and vandalizing the proud Pacific Heritage Monuments, the furious fusion of sea creature and mammal fought the Power Rangers and captured them in its magic jar. After the confrontation moved to the mountains, the remaining Rangers (Blue and Red) successfully freed their teammates by utilizing a mirror as a distraction against the vain villain. The Octophantom, capable of plentiful power, was destroyed once again by the combined might of the marvelous Thunder Megazord.

DESIGNATION
STAG BEETLE

YEAR	ORIGIN	TYPE
(2)		

Alias (Nickname)
Bug Brain

Known Abilities
Pincer Power,
Indestructible
Exoskeleton,
Power Drain

THE STONE CANYON YOUTH CENTER AND THE ANGEL GROVE YOUTH CENTER WERE DUE TO TAKE

part in a friendly game of broomball when the terrible Stag Beetle attacked Angel Grove. Though some claimed it was a coincidence that the Stone Canyon mascot was a beetle, it seemed that Zedd found inspiration for his new monster in the mascot itself. The Stag Beetle first appeared in the park, and later moved to the mountains, after successfully draining the Green Ranger of his powers. The Green Ranger later reappeared in a harrowing rescue as the Rangers were about to be blasted off a cliff by the advancing and seemingly undefeatable Stag Beetle. Utilizing a device created by Alpha 5, the Green Ranger dodged the antagonist's attack and reabsorbed his diminished powers. With powers regained, the Green Ranger rejoined the battle as his fellow Rangers formed the Power Blaster. This, unfortunately, had no effect on the Stag Beetle. Eventually, it lost its pincers at the edge of the Thunder Megazord's sword and fell to its explosive end soon after.

DESIGNATION
INVENUSABLE FLYTRAP

YEAR 2 **ORIGIN** **TYPE**

Alias (Nickname)
Weed
Known Abilities
Trap Chest,
Master of
Venus Island

THE INVENUSABLE FLYTRAP NEVER SET FOOT IN ANGEL GROVE. THIS CARNIVOROUS FLORA WAS

the master of a mysterious island located in the middle of the Atlantic Ocean. The reason for the Flytrap's inclusion is due to an abnormal abduction of one of Angel Grove's young citizens. This citizen, who wished to remain anonymous, later explained that a "terrifying golden monkey" (assumed to be Goldar) abducted her one day on the beach and took her to an inexplicable island somewhere in the center of the Atlantic Ocean. This island, rumored by conspiracy theorists to be called "Venus Island," allegedly appeared only when Lord Zedd called it into being. Trade winds flowed toward its location at sunset. Alpha 5 offered little information to corroborate this claim, although limited data does reveal that such an island exists. It was on this island that the Power Rangers allegedly battled and defeated the Invenusable Flytrap. Alpha 5's data also offers the means of the Flytrap's defeat: Having trapped the Rangers in its chest, they joined Power Coins to create an immense heat that the creature could not withstand. After the creature ejected them from its chest, the Rangers formed their Power Blaster and reduced the wicked weed to cinders.

DESIGNATION
GUITARDO

Alias (Nickname)
n/a
Known Abilities
Hypnotic Magic,
Eye-Beam
Projection

WHEN ROCK AND ROLL WAS FIRST INTRODUCED ON RADIOS AROUND THE UNITED STATES, MANY

concerned citizens believed the music was evil. While the fears subsided and rock and roll became a mainstay in popular music, Zedd's next monster proved that rock and roll could indeed be wicked. Guitardo, a creature similar in appearance to a cicada, utilized its magically enchanted guitar to play repulsive rock tunes that could control the minds of its victims. Guitardo was first witnessed by Bulk and Skull in Angel Grove Park, where the creature confronted the Power Rangers for the first time. One witness reported that the irritating insect began playing a song that caused the Rangers to suddenly be lifted into the air. With four Rangers out of the game and under Guitardo's musical spell, the Green Ranger and Pink Ranger finally faced down the cicada alien at the deserted Angel Grove Fairgrounds. Ultimately the Pink Ranger defeated Guitardo with the power of her bow and the Green Ranger's trusty Dragon Dagger.

TURBAN SHELL

Alias (Nickname)
Mollusk Brain
Known Abilities
Laser Eyes, Staff, Power-Draining Shell

"WE INTERRUPT THIS PROGRAM FOR A SPECIAL LIVE REPORT. LOCAL

government sources have confirmed that the creature known as Turban Shell has begun another assault on Angel Grove. The attack, at the moment confined to the business district downtown, comes less than twenty-four hours after its first attack was repulsed by the Power Rangers."

This was the newscast heard throughout Angel Grove on the day of the attack by Turban Shell, often remembered as one of the more damaging attacks on the city. This monstrous mollusk possessed a dangerously high level of power and aided in Zedd's attempt to destroy the Green Ranger. The creature's origins are largely unknown, though some suspect he was created from a mollusk living in Angel Grove Lake. Turban Shell first appeared in Angel Grove, towering over the city and destroying several buildings. Luckily, though with much difficulty, the Power Rangers managed to fight and defeat the monster by superheating him from within, spraying him with cold water from the outside, and shattering him with a strike of the Power Saber.

Alias (Nickname)
n/a
Known Abilities
Optical Energy
Blast, Prehensile
Pipes, Pipe Arm
with Teeth

PIPE BRAIN WAS, BY FAR, ONE OF THE MOST SHORT-LIVED AND ILL-CONCEIVED OF

Zedd's monsters, though he did prove to be a pest to the Red Ranger for a limited time. While Alpha 5's data proved inconclusive, it is commonly believed that the Pipe Brain monster was created from a trophy that went missing from the Golden Pipe Karate Competition at the Angel Grove Youth Center. Regardless, Pipe Brain originally appeared in the park, where the Red Ranger easily evaded its attacks, thus angering the impatient Zedd and causing the arrival of a growth bomb from the moon. Even after momentarily trapping the Red Ranger's Zord in an intense pipe-tentacle wrap, Pipe Brain proved weaker than his opponent and finally fell to the ground, defeated.

DESIGNATION

TRUMPET TOP

YEAR	ORIGIN	TYPE
2		

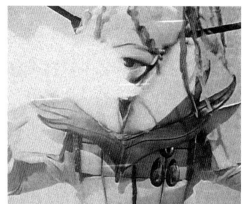

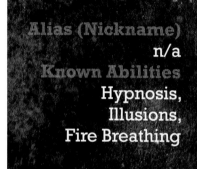

Alias (Nickname)
n/a
Known Abilities
Hypnosis,
Illusions,
Fire Breathing

CAPABLE OF CASTING MIND-ALTERING ILLUSIONS, TRUMPET TOP MADE THE POWER RANGERS

believe they were being attacked by an army of their ex-foes. Zedd created his newest musical monstrosity from another stolen item—a vintage trumpet belonging to a student at Angel Grove High— on the same day that a jazz performance was scheduled at the Angel Grove Youth Center. After appearing in the park, Trumpet Top hypnotized the recently arrived Power Rangers. To eyewitnesses, Bulk and Skull included, the Power Rangers seemed to be dazed. In their confusion, they fought nothing but the air before them.

"*They were just kicking and punching the air,*" Skull told a local reporter at the time. "*I mean, it was pretty cool. They got good moves, you know. But, yeah, there was nothing there.*"

According to Alpha 5's account of the encounter, the Rangers believed they were battling a barrage of bygone beasts: Saliguana, Fighting Flea, Soccadillo, Mantis, Rhino Blaster, and several other past enemies. After being alerted to the illusion by Zordon, the Rangers regrouped and defeated Trumpet Top with resounding success. The spell was broken, and the original trumpet returned to its rightful owner.

127

DESIGNATION
MIRROR MANIAC

Alias (Nickname)
n/a
Known Abilities
Mirror Blast

THE MADNESS OF THE MIRROR MANIAC WAS RETROSPECTIVELY OVERSHADOWED BY A

far more fascinating series of events that took place during the monster's brief time in Angel Grove. The Mirror Maniac, created from a run-of-the-mill pocket mirror, made a brief appearance during Lord Zedd's attempt to capture and marry the Pink Ranger. According to Alpha 5's data, Goldar was sent to fetch the Pink Ranger and return with her to Zedd's Cave of Fantasy. However, Goldar failed to convince the strong-willed Ranger with what little magic he had at his disposal. Eventually she was rescued by the Yellow and Blue Rangers, and the three Rangers joined the others to do battle against the Mirror Maniac in Angel Grove Park. While the Mirror Maniac proved a masterful monster, the Megazord quickly smashed the monster's glass and proceeded to slash the reflective surface with the mighty Saber. Zedd would later find a more appropriate associate to be his blushing bride.

NIMROD, THE SCARLET SENTINEL

YEAR	ORIGIN	TYPE
2	🌐	?

Alias (Nickname)
Lightning Rod
Known Abilities
Lightning
Projection,
Shoulder Lasers,
AC and DC

A NEW CHAPTER BEGAN WITH THE ARRIVAL OF NIMROD, THE SCARLET SENTINEL.

While Nimrod's attack on the city was memorable for many reasons, its appearance became the prelude to the introduction of a new and awesome Ranger—the White Ranger. According to Alpha 5's information, he and Zordon had retreated to an unknown location for unknown reasons, and Lord Zedd had sensed their absence. Zedd cast a spell on the Sentinel Statue (a giant marble fist) in the park, which began its transformation into Nimrod. While the monster developed, green slime began to cover the statue, and locals soon took notice. Around the same time, a miraculous meteor was reported flying through the skies of Angel Grove by none other than Bulk and Skull. The pair took the found meteor back to Skull's workshop and began to open the extraterrestrial item. Meanwhile, back in the park, the Sentinel Statue burst into flames. From these flames burst Nimrod, the Scarlet Sentinel. Grown large by Zedd, Nimrod produced her two companions, AC and DC, who proceeded to attack the industrial center of Angel Grove. At this time, the miraculous appearance of the White Ranger occurred. He battled his overgrown opponents with the aid of the new White Tigerzord and, after a brief struggle, emerged victorious. A new age was declared in Angel Grove, and a new Ranger joined the team.

PURSEHEAD AND LIPSYNCHER

Alias (Nickname)
Bag Head
Known Abilities
Pursehead:
Compact Ray,
Floss Bind
Lipsyncher: Sword,
Powerful
Sound Waves

THE DIABOLICAL DUO KNOWN AS PURSEHEAD AND LIPSYNCHER WERE CREATED FROM A PURSE AND A TUBE OF LIPSTICK. THE SUDDEN CREATION OF TWO MONSTERS

by Lord Zedd caused the Rangers to divide and conquer. Pursehead was the first to appear in the park, where she froze the White and Pink Rangers in their tracks with the use of a compact ray (similar to a mirror). In coming to their rescue, the Black Ranger also received the "cold shoulder," winding up frozen just like the other two. Lipsyncher later appeared and was immediately challenged by the Red Ranger, who left a noticeable gash on the freakish fiend's face. Upset by the blow to her beauty, Lipsyncher grew (at the command of Zedd) and entered into a severe struggle with the Red Ranger's Zord. Soon after Red's battle had begun, the Blue Ranger returned to the scene of Pursehead's attack and freed his fellow Rangers with a newly developed reverse ocular dilator. The remaining Rangers joined the Red Ranger in his battle against the overgrown

Lipsyncher. The White Ranger remained behind to battle the petulant Pursehead. After being tossed around by Pursehead's effective floss bind, the White Ranger's companion Saber zapped the hazardous handbag and returned it to its original state. The combined efforts of the rest of the Rangers against the towering Lipsyncher proved fruitful as the colossal cosmetic monster fell fast under their power.

DESIGNATION
MAGNET BRAIN

Alias (Nickname)
n/a
Known Abilities
Polarity Staff,
Magnetic Beam

A RARE SOLAR STORM WAS PREDICTED FOR ANGEL GROVE ON THE DAY THAT ZEDD CREATED

Magnet Brain. According to Alpha 5's data, the Blue Ranger, a scientist at heart, had created a "polarizer" to record the effects of the solar storm. Catching wind of the device, Zedd sent Goldar and a gang of Putties to steal the polarizer. Once retrieved, Zedd sent a beam of lightning from his staff to transform the scientific instrument into the magnetic miscreant known as Magnet Brain. According to several shaken eyewitnesses, the electric enemy threw its staff into the air, which instantly caused a severe disruption of Earth's magnetic poles, which were momentarily thrown into chaos, causing Earth to shift out of its natural rotation. The effects were felt throughout the world, but Angel Grove citizens held on tightly as the ground beneath them shifted. The Rangers arrived in the industrial district to confront Magnet Brain, who, with his staff, caused the Blade Blasters to backfire. Within moments, a growth bomb arrived and left the magnetic monster towering above the city's tallest buildings. Using a gigantic magnet, the monster momentarily impeded the Megazord. However, the Megazord responded by tearing the creature in half, leading to its destruction.

KEY MONSTER
AND DOOMSTONE

YEAR	ORIGIN	TYPE
2	?	◻

Alias (Nickname)
n/a
Known Abilities
Key Monster: Key to the Dark Dimension
Doomstone: Resurrection

FORTUNATELY, THE CITIZENS OF ANGEL GROVE NEVER HAD TO WITNESS THE

two terrors known as Key Monster and Doomstone. The Angel Grove Youth Center had organized a quaint Halloween event for the local children, entertaining them and supplying them with a trick-or-treating experience while their parents went about their day. It just so happened to be the first Halloween in Angel Grove during Zedd's reign on the moon. According to Alpha 5's data, Zedd thought it thrilling to throw his first Dark Dimension Monster Bash with the White Ranger as his special guest. After Goldar trapped and transported the White Ranger to the Dark Dimension via the Key Monster, the lone Ranger was met by tombstones and a thick fog. Shortly after, Doomstone entered the scene and proceeded to "resurrect" an assortment of angry antagonists. Robogoat, Primator, Rhino Blaster, the Snizzard, and the Pumpkin Rapper (among others) were brought back to battle the trapped White Ranger. However, not long after the White Ranger's arrival, his fellow Rangers appeared to destroy the resurrected wrongdoers and return to Earth unharmed.

TERROR BLOSSOM

YEAR	ORIGIN	TYPE
②		

Alias (Nickname)
n/a
Known Abilities
Poisonous Petals

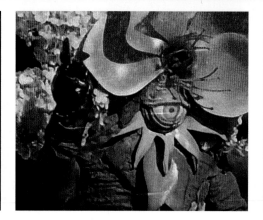

AN EERIE WIND SWEPT THROUGH THE CITY AS FLOWER PETALS FROM

from the trees and ground were blown around in a whirlwind of pink and yellow. As the multicolored petals converged, a bolt of lightning from the moon struck the tiny tornado. From the mysterious maelstrom of petals and lightning emerged the elegant and trim Terror Blossom. The floral foe soon sent poisonous petals pouring through Angel Grove. Moments later the Red, Yellow, and Black Rangers would arrive to find the flower calling upon an old foe—Hatchasaurus. While Hatchasaurus distracted the Rangers, the Terror Blossom set about on his search for a heat source to germinate his seed pods and replicate himself. Once Hatchasaurus was destroyed, the Rangers returned to find Terror Blossom on a rampage. An ill-conceived confrontation left the Red, Yellow, and Black Rangers frozen by the Blossom's poisonous petals. As the boisterous Blossom made his way toward the local power plant, the Blue Ranger succeeded in freeing his friends. Together, the combined force of the Rangers stopped the monster in his tracks. Even after an attempt by Zedd to aid his newest creation, Terror Blossom was mowed over by the combined might of the Thunder Megazord and the White Tigerzord.

FOUR HEAD

Alias (Nickname)
n/a
Known Abilities
Staff

THE ANNUAL WORLD TEEN SUMMIT WAS HELD AT THE ANGEL GROVE YOUTH CENTER

with foreign dignitaries from around the world in attendance. For this special occasion, the Angel Grove High School art class sculpted a special statue with four heads representing wisdom, beauty, strength, and vitality. Following the initial events at the Youth Center, foreign friends were then treated to a view of the park by several high-school students. It was there that Goldar and a platoon of Putties appeared and snatched away the terrified travelers. Bulk and Skull relayed to me that they stalked Goldar as he led the abductees to a cave in the mountains outside the city. As Bulk and Skull prepared to save the tourists, the Power Rangers arrived and did the job for them. Lord Zedd, in turn, responded with rage, transforming the four-headed statue into the fearsome Four Head! The Rangers soon combined weapons to form the Power Blaster, but this had no effect on the curious creation. Once grown by Zedd's magic and towering over the city, Four Head posed a problem that would be abruptly solved upon the arrival of a new Zord—Tor, the Carrierzord. This heavy, tank-like turtle Zord combined with the Megazord to form the Thunder Ultrazord and proceeded to deal a lethal blow to the beast briefly known as Four Head.

BEAMCASTER

Alias (Nickname)
n/a
Known Abilities
Mind Control,
Apple and Frog
Bombs

A DISGRUNTLED DISC JOCKEY WITH MIND-CONTROLLING AIRWAVES WAS NOT WHAT

attendees of the Stone Canyon Triathlon expected as they prepared for the grueling competition. A near success for Lord Zedd, the appearance of the Beamcaster created quite a stir around the Angel Grove lake and park area as spectators suddenly fell under the spell of Zedd Waves. These sinister sound waves, created and distributed by Beamcaster, caused anyone who heard them to fall into a deep trance. In the local news, following the encounter, several witnesses (unaffected due to wearing headphones) described the individuals in the park as having "turned into zombies, man!" The Power Rangers also fell victim to the Beamcaster's sound waves after arriving and briefly attempting to subdue the resonating rogue. After being awakened from their hypnosis by some mysterious circumstance, the Rangers rallied as they had so many times before. The team formed their Power Blaster and broke the spell by blowing up the beast.

DESIGNATION

SILVER HORNS

YEAR	ORIGIN	TYPE
2		

Alias (Nickname)
Tick Face

Known Abilities
Bug Bombs,
Electric Beams,
Powerful Pincers

A STRANGE SERIES OF EVENTS PRECEDED THE ARRIVAL OF THE

horrible giant tick known as Silver Horns. A machine sent to Earth by Lord Zedd floated above the ground in Angel Grove Park. Noxious fumes were released from the machine, which caused a colossal cloud to blanket the city and render its residents unconscious. During this period, no Power Rangers could be found. As the cloud continued on its path, taking more and more victims, the machine was somehow destroyed. When the citizens of Angel Grove awoke from their sleep, they found Silver Horns rampaging through the city. The Rangers' arrival did not allay fears as the terrible tick tossed bug bombs and released electrical shocks from his horned head. Soon, Silver Horns towered over the mountains as a storm formed over the city. The skies grew dark and lightning erupted all around as Serpentera, Zedd's shocking serpent Zord, arrived and stood over Angel Grove. While Serpentera made no actions against the city, the presence of Zedd's Zord made the defeat of Silver Horns by the Power Rangers bittersweet. As Serpentera flew away, the citizens of Angel Grove knew for certain that it would return.

DESIGNATION

SKELERENA

Alias (Nickname)
Bone Brain
Known Abilities
Obnoxious and
Consistent
Laughter

WHAT SKELERENA LACKED IN POWERS, HE MADE UP FOR IN SHEER ANNOYANCE.

First appearing in the park, this horrendous, skeletal hyena hybrid was spotted running swiftly through the trees, howling with laughter as it moved. Eventually, it emerged onto a crowded sidewalk where pedestrians enjoying a pleasant afternoon stroll were met with the brain-and-bone-rattling cackle of Zedd's newest creation. As Skelerena continued to terrorize the panic-stricken citizens of Angel Grove, the Power Rangers arrived and were met by a pack of Putties. Skelerena stood at the edge of the park, enjoying the view of the ensuing battle. With the arrival of the Rangers, Skelerena began jumping through the air and rolling about laughing. The Rangers produced their new weapon, the Power Cannon, which ended the brief yet terrible reign of Skelerena.

SCATTERBRAIN

Alias (Nickname)
Yellow-Bellied
Skunk
Known Abilities
Kaleidoscope Ray,
Sword

CREATED FROM A STANDARD KALEIDOSCOPE BY LORD ZEDD,

Scatterbrain wielded a power unlike anything Angel Grove had seen before. In its first encounter with the Power Rangers, the killer kaleidoscope shot a multicolored beam from its head that hit several of the Power Rangers, causing complete memory loss. Fortunately, the Blue Ranger managed to scrounge up a prism, which would cause Scatterbrain's kaleidoscope ray to have the opposite effect. Returning to battle Scatterbrain, the Blue Ranger utilized the prism to great success, restoring the memories of his mystified mates. Scatterbrain then entered into a duel of swords with the Thunder Megazord, which, thankfully, ended with Scatterbrain's kaleidoscope brain destroyed. Bulk and Skull seemed to believe that they played a significant role in this encounter, though this cannot be confirmed or denied.

DESIGNATION
PACHINKO HEAD

YEAR	ORIGIN	TYPE
2		

Alias (Nickname)

Metalhead

Known Abilities

Transforming Ball Blast, Optical Energy Beam

PACHINKO, A POPULAR ARCADE GAME ORIGINATING IN JAPAN, WAS THE

inspiration for another of Zedd's chaotic creations. Ernie, owner of the Angel Grove Youth Center, had recently acquired an attractive Pachinko machine for his Juice Bar. However, Lord Zedd caught wind of the purchase and transformed the stolen machine into the fearsome mechanical freak known as Pachinko Head. This arcade antagonist used his pachinko ball blast to turn all but one Power Ranger into oversize pachinko balls. The White Ranger, having avoided the blast, confronted Pachinko Head at the local amusement park, where the monster had caused a spinning ride to spin dangerously fast. Zedd arrived on Earth soon after in his colossal Serpentera Zord and grew Pachinko Head to magnificent size. Fortunately, Pachinko Head was defeated by the Power Rangers and their superior Zords. Serpentera attempted to take them on but, once they were joined by Tor, fell victim to another devastating and lethal blow.

DESIGNATION
SHOWBIZ MONSTER

Alias (Nickname)
Mindless Mass of
Metal and Glass
Known Abilities
n/a

EVERY SCENE WAS A FIGHT SCENE FOR LORD ZEDD'S NEXT

creation, Showbiz Monster. Out to make a name for himself in the business of extraterrestrial invaders by once and for all destroying the Power Rangers, the Showbiz Monster didn't quite make the cut. The Power Rangers appeared for the first time on national television via the *Harvey Garvey Show* and were officially welcomed by worldwide audiences.

"*You've come to know them and love them as superheroes battling against unbeatable odds,*" Mr. Garvey announced. "*Fighting monsters of all shapes and sizes. Protecting us from the forces of evil. They are proponents of good will and brotherly love and here they are in their first television appearance as the worldwide ambassadors . . . ladies and gentlemen, boys and girls, the one and only Mighty Morphin Power Rangers!*"

Zedd, annoyed with the attention the Rangers were getting, zapped a television camera. The ensuing monster, the Showbiz Monster, instantly appeared on a bridge in the park. The Showbiz beast was quickly met by the Rangers' Zords, who proved once again that they are indeed protecting the world from the forces of evil.

DESIGNATION

FLAME HEAD

YEAR
2

ORIGIN

TYPE

Alias (Nickname)
Match Stick
Known Abilities
Fire Breath,
Flame Sword

LORD ZEDD CREATED FLAME HEAD IN A DIABOLICAL EFFORT TO MAKE ANGEL GROVE

the hottest place on Earth. Bulk and Skull were in the park when the blazing bad guy arrived on the back of a white horse and set fire to a family barbecue. A trash can behind Bulk and Skull was also set ablaze, leading to their inevitable escape from the monster and winding up in the lake. Flame Head then set about igniting trees, tables, and anything else he could manage. After riding violently through the forest, he was met by the Rangers, whom he threatened to turn into "French toast." Soon after, the Rangers set out to extinguish the fiendish fire freak! After dodging and weaving away from the monster's flame breath and sword, the Rangers and their Zords finally (and literally) extinguished the threat of Flame Head. A simple fire extinguisher was all it took to douse his flames for good.

CANNONTOP

Alias (Nickname)

Barrel Head

Known Abilities

Chest, Head, and Shoulder Cannons (a lot of cannons)

LORD ZEDD SENT CANNONTOP, CREATED FROM A TOY CANNON FOUND IN THE PARK,

to Angel Grove with the intent of blasting its citizens into an intergalactic dimension of no return. This dimension, reportedly called the Lost Dimension, was opened during this encounter by Lord Zedd himself. Fortunately, due to the bravery of the Power Rangers, Zedd's plan never came to fruition and the Rangers remained in their own dimension. However disappointed Lord Zedd must have been in his failure (once again), his Cannontop monster actually put up a good fight when faced with the overwhelming power of the superhuman squad of Rangers. Appearing in the park, Cannontop utilized every cannon available in his arsenal in an attempt to topple the mighty morphin heroes. Yet, even after utilizing his shoulder cannons (and a double blast from the main cannon), the explosive enemy fell short in his ability to actually *hit* his target. In the end, after being grown by Lord Zedd in a last-ditch effort to make his monster a success, Cannontop met a sudden and fiery end at the wrong end of the Mega Tigerzord's attack.

WELDO

Alias (Nickname)
n/a
Known Abilities
Weldo: Optical
Energy Blast
Evil Bookala:
Tentacle Tongue

MUCH OF THE FOLLOWING EVENT TOOK PLACE IN CLOSE QUARTERS AND INVOLVED PRIVATE INTERACTIONS BETWEEN THE POWER RANGERS IN

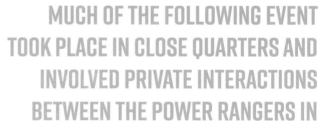

their supposed civilian identities. As such, the information provided is largely based on hearsay, rumor, and what small bit of information was provided by Alpha 5's documents. The day began with the appearance of the first, and potentially normal, UFO sighting over Angel Grove. The unidentified flying object fell from the sky over the park and was recovered by unnamed citizens (presumed to be the Power Rangers). This craft, according to Alpha 5's information, came from the planet Bookala, carrying a rare lightning diamond as its energy source. The Bookala (an alien named after the planet) within the ship had been evading Lord Zedd, who wished to obtain the diamond to power his Serpentera Zord. When the Bookala (both ship

EVIL BOOKALA

YEAR	ORIGIN	TYPE
2	?	?

and occupant) evaded capture, Zedd created the monster Weldo. Weldo, however, was quickly defeated by the Power Rangers. Moments later, after the Bookala ship left Earth, an Evil Bookala appeared and grew to towering heights. Although briefly ensnared by the Evil Bookala's disgusting, tentacle-like tongue, the Rangers' Zords emerged victorious. Alpha 5's data also makes a note that the true Bookala from the planet Bookala was actually incredibly friendly and an example that other extraterrestrials should follow.

JAWS OF DESTRUCTION

YEAR	ORIGIN	TYPE
②		

Alias (Nickname)
Tool Shop Reject
Known Abilities
Sawblade Swords

LORD ZEDD'S MONSTROUS CREATURE, JAWS OF DESTRUCTION, KEPT THE CITIZENS OF

Angel Grove on the razor's edge of anticipation. Jaws of Destruction was created from a stolen hacksaw that went missing from the Angel Grove High School woodworking shop around the same time as the encounter. Regardless, at the same time as the Jaws attack, a local student interested in gymnastics was also reportedly abducted by Goldar. How these two events are connected is a mystery. After the monster appeared in the park and was witnessed by Bulk and Skull (as always), the Power Rangers arrived and battled the sharp-tongued titan, who eventually grew thanks to a perfectly timed growth bomb. As the sun set on the city, the Rangers and their Zords struck down the metal maniac with a devastating blow of the Saber. The abducted innocent was returned safe and sound by the ever-heroic Rangers.

DESIGNATION

TUBE MONSTER
AND THE RISE OF THE SEA MONSTERS

YEAR	ORIGIN	TYPE
2		

Alias (Nickname)
Tuna Breath
Known Abilities
n/a

ONE NEW MONSTER AND FOUR OLD ADVERSARIES PLAGUED THE POWER

Rangers on a fine summer afternoon. The Angel Grove Beach was full of fresh-faced young friends and families who were enjoying the mild heat and soothing sounds of the waves lapping at the sand. The fun, unfortunately, came to an end with the return of several slime-covered sea monsters who emerged on the beach and began wreaking havoc. The sinister Slippery Shark appeared first, followed by Goo Fish, the unpleasant Pirantishead, and the contemptible Commander Crayfish. The Power Rangers arrived within moments, and the fishy fiends fought violently to make up for their previous failures. It was a fair fight until Lord Zedd, sensing defeat, created a new monster with the sole purpose of dividing the Power Rangers. The Tube Monster, created from Bulk and Skull's inflatable inner tube, grasped a growth bomb and began attacking downtown Angel Grove. The White Ranger remained to vanquish the sea monsters while the rest of the Rangers returned to the city to destroy their inflatable foe. As the White Ranger finished off the resurrected rascals, Bulk and Skull's inner tube reappeared in the water, signaling the defeat of the temporary Tube Monster.

DESIGNATION
PHOTOMARE

YEAR	ORIGIN	TYPE
2	🌐	⚡

Alias (Nickname)
n/a
Known Abilities
Photo-Capture
Camera

ZEDD'S CRAZED CAMERA CREATION ARRIVED DURING A VERY STRANGE TIME

in Angel Grove. The following events are largely speculation as the events of this day are essentially absent from the minds of those who experienced them.

The Rock of Time, an ancient artifact with time-warping capabilities, came into Lord Zedd's possession. With this strange stone, Zedd managed to reverse the rotation of our planet, thus causing all of its inhabitants to age backward. Effectively, Zedd turned back time on Earth. Citizens of the world were reduced in age by many years, some blinking out of existence altogether. During this time, Zedd created the Photomare, capable of freezing folks in photos forever. While the fiendish Photomare caused panic in the park, eventually the Rangers arrived to fight the villain. They made quick work of dismantling Photomare before moving to the mountains. It was there that they were rumored to have fought off a flock of frightening monsters before destroying the Rock of Time and returning Earth to its natural place in space and time.

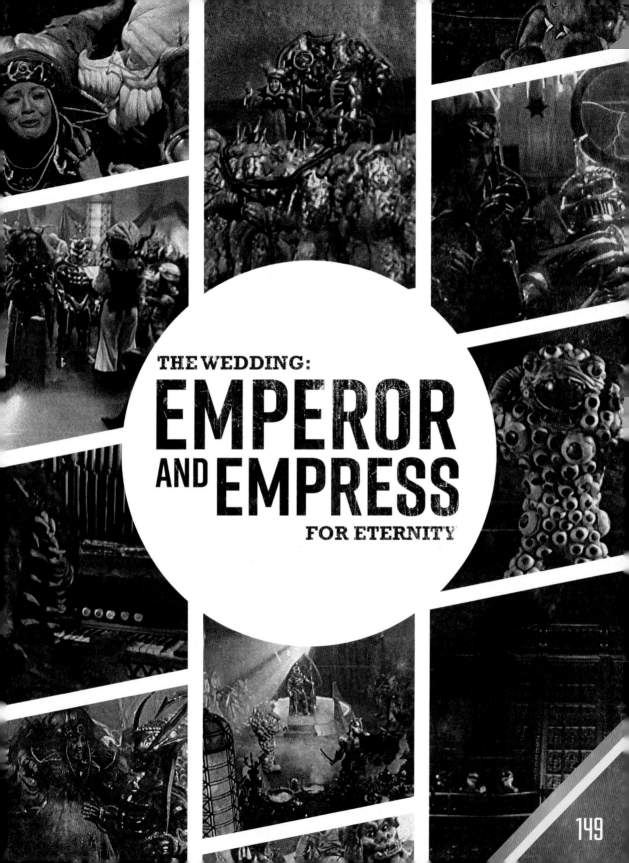

THE WEDDING:
EMPEROR
AND EMPRESS
FOR ETERNITY

DURING THEIR CONTINUED QUEST FOR WORLD DOMINATION, LORD ZEDD AND RITA REPULSA FOUND THE TIME TO THROW AN EXTRAVAGANT AND EVIL WEDDING. WHILE WEDDINGS ARE NORMALLY A JOYOUS OCCASION FOR THE CITIZENS OF PLANET EARTH, THE BINDING TOGETHER OF TWO TERRIBLE FOES WAS NOT A SIGN OF GOOD THINGS TO COME.

And like all encounters with Lord Zedd and Rita Repulsa, the story of their evil nuptials had unexpected and nefarious beginnings. When Lord Zedd arrived at the Moon Palace, his first order of business was to lock Rita Repulsa away in her drab space dumpster as punishment for her continued defeat at the hands of his enemies. She was to be banished, cast out into the darkest corner of the galaxy. After assuming control of the palace once more, Lord Zedd mounted further failed attempts at the destruction of Angel Grove and found that the Power Rangers were not as easily defeated as he had surely suspected. Unbeknownst to Zedd, the Empress of Evil had successfully found her way back from her banishment and was out for revenge. Finster, Rita's ever-faithful monster maker, successfully returned his mistress from her miniature size (shrunken to about six inches in order to fit within the dumpster) back to her normal stature. According to Alpha 5's data, Rita demanded two things from Finster:

1. CRAFT A LOVE POTION CAPABLE OF MAKING LORD ZEDD FALL IN LOVE WITH HER.

2. HELP HER DESTROY THE POWER RANGERS ONCE AND FOR ALL.

Arriving on Earth near the Command Center, Finster and several Putties surprised Alpha 5 outside. Finster inserted a new program into the loyal automaton's system and fled back to the moon to begin creating the love potion. Alpha 5, now evilly inclined due to the invasion of his circuitry, returned to the Command Center and proceeded with the plan that Finster had implanted. Alpha 5 notes in his data that this was, perhaps, the most frightening experience of his existence. Blocking Zordon from communication with the Power Rangers, Alpha 5 sent out an emergency alert demanding that the Rangers quickly get to the abandoned Spectre Theater outside of Angel Grove. Once there, they were met with locked doors and a horde of

old foes who had been resurrected by Finster. The theater had also been transformed into a vortex via Rita's evil magic, cutting off the Rangers' vital power source. With no contact to Zordon, Alpha 5 under an evil influence, and a drain on their powers, the Power Rangers were on the verge of defeat.

BACK ON THE MOON, RITA ENTERED ZEDD'S CHAMBER AND FED THE LOVE POTION DIRECTLY INTO ZEDD'S VEINS.

She woke him prematurely from his Centennial Recharge and found that the potion had worked—Lord Zedd had fallen madly in love with her. Finster had succeeded, and so, too, had Rita. The evil Lord of the Moon proposed on the spot, leaving Goldar, Squatt, and Baboo in charge of pulling together a sudden and, ultimately, unsatisfactory wedding.

Back on Earth, the Power Rangers had luckily discovered a cave beneath the theater and managed to escape. The fleeing friends were met in the mountains by massive monsters that had been sized up by Lord Zedd's infamous growth bombs. Not only was there a wedding planned, but Rita also had seemingly served up the Rangers on a silver platter for her groom-to-be.

Alpha 5, still under Finster's control, cut off all energy to the Zords and teleported the Rangers back to the theater. Their Zords, abandoned in the mountains, quickly fell to the might of the overgrown Rhino Blaster and Peckster. Soon after, the two monsters returned to normal size and arrived at the theater to watch over the Rangers while the marriage unfolded upon the moon.

WITH MANY MONSTERS IN ATTENDANCE AND A BEASTLY BANQUET LAID OUT, RITA AND ZEDD PLEDGED THEIR LOVE TO EACH OTHER AND SHARED A GRUESOME KISS AS PROOF OF THEIR EVERLASTING EVIL.

Finster performed the ceremony, and the Snizzard, enchanted by further magic, played the piano while the new Mister and Missus of the Moon danced among their monstrous minions. Several eyewitnesses on Earth claim to have seen fireworks or bright lights over the moon during this time, but I have not been able to either confirm or deny this occurrence.

As the party drew to an end, Rita and Zedd saddled up in Serpentera to begin their honeymoon with a most wonderful event—the destruction of the Power Rangers. The Power Rangers, having once again escaped the theater, ran across the barren landscape of the mountains outside of the city toward the Command Center. However, they were halted by a group of towering terrors. As Serpentera passed in front of the moon, Goldar sent a horde of monsters to the mountains in order to finally get rid of the rascally Rangers. Saliguana, Robogoat, Dramole, Grumble Bee, Soccadillo, and Eye Guy, all grown and vicious, charged forward and were quickly met by the arrival of the Rangers' Zords. Unbeknownst to their foes, the Rangers had moments earlier arrived at the Command Center and removed the invasive disc from Alpha 5's system, thus restoring him and his powers. With Zordon and Alpha 5 back online, the Power Rangers and their Zords led a brilliant battle against the ferocious freaks who meant to end them for all time. While Rita and Zedd had hoped to off the Power Rangers for their honeymoon, the couple returned to the moon having once again witnessed another astonishing defeat.

WIZARD OF DECEPTION

YEAR	ORIGIN	TYPE
2		

Alias (Nickname)
Lizard Dude
Known Abilities
Wizard:
Mind Control,
Time Travel
Rat Monsters:
Giant Rat Powers

THE POWER RANGERS' FIRST FORAY INTO TIME TRAVEL INVOLVED A WICKED WIZARD OF DECEPTION AND HIS CREATIONS, KNOWN ONLY AS RAT MONSTERS.

Summoned to Earth by Rita Repulsa with the help of a powerful, disembodied skull known as the Ghost of Darkness, the Wizard of Deception first made a clone of the Green Ranger and transported the Power Rangers back in time to the late 1700s. Several uncovered historical documents preserved by the Angel Grove Historical Society reveal that early settlers in Angel Grove were one day alarmed by the sudden arrival of "witches" (presumably the Power Rangers). An attack by a "cloaked, masked wizard" soon followed, whereupon the wizard used his "magic staff" to transform several small rats into "hideous, man-size rat monsters." According to legend, the Wizard of Deception then began randomly blowing up the surrounding area, including "houses, carriages, and a small assortment of barrels" in an attempt to defeat the Rangers. His disappearance was

RAT MONSTERS

YEAR
2

ORIGIN

TYPE

only eclipsed by the giant rats he left behind.

Back in the present day, the evil Green Ranger clone had awakened the Dragonzord from its slumber in the murky depths to initiate an attack on Angel Grove. Fortunately, the other Rangers intervened and successfully destroyed the Wizard of Deception. The Dragonzord was returned to the ocean. Nothing is certain regarding the whereabouts of the mysterious clone. Legend says that Angel Grove of the 1700s was supposedly saved by a stranger in green.

TURKEY JERK

Alias (Nickname)
Pathetic Piece
of Poultry

Known Abilities
Baster Blaster

BULK AND SKULL WERE LARGELY RESPONSIBLE FOR THE CREATION OF THE TURKEY JERK.

After finding a copy of a book titled *Monster Making Made Easy* by H. P. Toth (largely suspected to be an alias of Finster), Bulk and Skull set about making the monster in their garage lab. Their intention, confirmed to me by Bulk, was to create a monster that would draw out the Power Rangers and discover their true identities once and for all. To safeguard against Bulk and Skull's scientific shortcomings, Zedd made sure that the monster came to life by casting down a bolt of lightning from his staff. The Turkey Jerk rose and Bulk and Skull quickly lost control of the beast and fled. The Rangers soon arrived to battle the pathetic poultry in the park, where they quickly clipped its wings and rid the city of this temporary terror.

MONDO THE MAGICIAN

YEAR	ORIGIN	TYPE
2	🌐	☆

Alias (Nickname)
Moth-Eaten
Magician
Known Abilities
Sword, Spell
Casting

MONDO THE MAGICIAN MADE HIS MARK ON THE CITY WITH PERHAPS THE STRANGEST ORIGIN

story of all. According to Alpha 5's limited data regarding this event, Mondo's mysterious appearance somehow resulted in half of the Power Rangers being magically transported into an illustrated storybook titled *Grumble: The Magic Elf*. In the book, the character Grumble has been put under a grumpy spell by a terrible magician in the mountains known as Mondo. While Grumble desires nothing more than to deliver toys to orphans, the arrival of the Rangers to his story and an attack by Putties forced the gentle creature to assist in the fight. Eventually, the Rangers escaped the book, but were followed by the evil Mondo with the help of Rita Repulsa. After exiting *Grumble: The Magic Elf*, the storybook sorcerer proceeded to the mountains where he briefly battled the Power Rangers before being written out of his final adventure.

157

NEEDLENOSE

Alias (Nickname)
Dainty Dandelion
Known Abilities
Paralyzing Spores,
Cactus Bombs

TIME TRAVEL ONCE AGAIN ASSISTED LORD ZEDD IN HIS DEVIOUS DEALINGS WITH THE POWER

Rangers. And while his creation known as Needlenose appeared briefly in present-day Angel Grove, the majority of his prickly practices took place around 1880. Once again, I have the Angel Grove Historical Society to thank for their comprehensive data catalogs and stories of the past. Unlike the Wizard of Deception's attack on Angel Grove in 1770, Needlenose arrived completely unannounced, accompanied by Goldar and a Putty Patrol. A Time Hole, supposedly having opened somewhere in or around the Youth Center, allowed them access to the past, and Zedd utilized the opportunity by attempting to destroy the city before it had even formed. He would have been successful had it not been for the supposed arrival of perhaps the first Power Rangers to ever call Angel Grove their home. According to Alpha 5, these "Rangers of 1880" were presented with the Power Coins after a plea to Alpha and Zordon, from the time-displaced Pink Ranger. It was with these Western Power Rangers that the Pink Ranger defeated Needlenose and Goldar, sending them back to their own time (ours) and saving the town from destruction. Back in the present, Needlenose was quickly dispatched by the current standing Power Rangers. Whether or not 1880 saw the first appearance of the Power Rangers is unknown as of yet.

DESIGNATION

VASE FACE

YEAR
2

ORIGIN

TYPE

Alias (Nickname)
Art Project
Known Abilities
Sword, Electric Snares, Laser Eyes

TERRIFYING AND MYSTERIOUS IN APPEARANCE, VASE FACE SPENT VERY

little time on Earth and had no real effect on the city of Angel Grove. Prior to the arrival of Vase Face, Lord Zedd and Rita Repulsa had successfully cloned another of the Rangers—the Blue Ranger. Alpha's data shows little information about this event, which leads one to assume that the cloning situation involved the true identity of the Blue Ranger, which is not to be revealed. Regardless, the cloning of the Blue Ranger coincided with the arrival of Vase Face, created by Lord Zedd from an Angel Grove High School art project. The amplified art project turned ceramic scoundrel attempted an attack on Angel Grove before being met by the cumulative force of the Power Rangers and their Zords. Armed with a sword, Vase Face battled our spirited celebrity saviors on the outskirts of the city. Eventually, and with much fanfare, the Power Rangers succeeded in shattering the brief bad guy known as Vase Face.

159

YEAR THREE

(1995–1996)

FAMILY REUNION

PART ONE

ULTIMATE EVIL

THE SECOND SWITCH-UP
THE FATHER (IN-LAW) OF ALL EVIL

Rita released monsters made by her ever-faithful Finster. Zedd created monsters made from the very materials of our planet. The second switch-up brought a new dynasty of evil, far more ancient and unknown than had been witnessed before. First came the camouflaged skeleton warrior. Next, the terrible Tengas and their furious flights across the skies. No one could have anticipated the arrival of Master Vile and his monstrous Skull Craft, which, when viewed in the sky, filled the people of Angel Grove with a terror most unexpected. Appearing and disappearing with luminescent slithering snakes, Master Vile ushered in a whole new era that stands out among previous attempts to attain ownership of Earth.

DESIGNATION
RITO REVOLTO

Alias (Nickname)
Rita's Brother
Known Abilities
Arm Cannon,
Sword,
Eager to Please

**ALPHA 5'S
MENACE
METER**

▶ Run. Please, run.

Take Cover.

Keep Away.

Mostly Harmless.

> ## "Monster? What? Oh! Right! The monster! You got it, Ed! No problemo! Everything is right on schedule. Count on it!"

A HELMETED BAG-OF-BONES, RITO REVOLTO, JOINED THE MOTLEY CREW IN THE MOON PALACE SOON AFTER THE WEDDING OF RITA REPULSA AND LORD ZEDD.

The sinister skeleton with a secret past arrived via an asteroid that struck the surface of the moon with such intensity that it was felt on Earth. Soon after his arrival in the Moon Palace, Rita recognized the bony barbarian as her brother. While there was no resemblance between the two, their actions toward each other clearly identified them as siblings. Rita relished her brother's place at the Moon Palace, yet constantly bickered with him and treated him like any other lackey. Rito, in turn, accepted his treatment by Rita, knowing that without her, Lord Zedd would have disposed of him quickly. Lord Zedd did not appreciate Rito's sudden arrival and continued to display apparent dislike for the boneheaded brother

of his wife. Being brother-in-law to one of the biggest forces of evil in the galaxy has its advantages, yet Rito seemed to disregard the stature of his sister's chosen partner. According to Alpha 5's inside intelligence, Rito took to calling Zedd "Ed," much to the Master of Evil's displeasure. With the whereabouts of Scorpina unknown, Rito took on the role of Goldar's partner in villainous deeds done on Earth.

Rito earned somewhat of a bad reputation for being a bumbling bonehead incapable of achieving simple sinister tasks. Yet in his first encounter in Angel Grove, Rito succeeded in a way that others before him had not. The skeleton managed the complete destruction of the Power Rangers' Zords, which fell, exploded, and burned up at the edge of the city. It is important to discuss the progression of events that led to the sad destruction of the Zords.

UPON ARRIVING AT THE MOON PALACE, RITO PRESENTED RITA AND ZEDD WITH A GIFT THAT WOULD MARK A NEW ERA FOR ATTACKS IN ANGEL GROVE. THE GIFT, GIVEN AS A WEDDING PRESENT, WAS A LARGE COLLECTION OF OVERSIZE EGGS, WHICH HE PLANTED IN THE DUST OUTSIDE OF THE PALACE AND CLOSER TO THE CLIFFS.

Initially, Rito could not recall precisely what the eggs contained. On later reflection, he revealed them to be a flock of crow-like monstrous minions known as Tenga Warriors (who will be discussed further in the following pages).

THE ACCIDENTAL REVELATION OF RITA'S LOVE (POTION)

The fact that Rita made Lord Zedd fall in love with her using a magic potion was a secret held between herself and her faithful monster maker, Finster. Somehow Rito uncovered the truth about the potion. Though Goldar had been suspicious all along, it was ultimately revealed that Lord Zedd *had* actually fallen in love with the Space Witch and the potion had worn off long ago.

On receipt of this gift, Lord Zedd sent Rito to Earth to lead a pack of monsters to destroy the Power Rangers. Octophantom, Fighting Flea, Stag Beetle, and the Lizzinator hid among the trees while Rito remained out in the open. Soon after, the Power Rangers arrived and were ambushed by Rito and his mob of monstrous meanies. Rita and Zedd aided the fight with their powerful magic that turned Rito and the monsters giant. Towering over the park, Rito attempted to stomp the Rangers underfoot.

Seeing that their battle had elevated, the Power Rangers called upon their Zords and the battle moved to the edge of the city. Rito countered attacks from all angles—falling only once or twice. With the Zords outnumbered, the monsters each delivered dangerous strikes followed by a baleful blast that ended the Zords' attempt at retaliation. Abandoning their posts, the Power Rangers woefully watched as their mechanical companions fell before their very eyes. The explosions rocked and reverberated throughout the city as hope suddenly seemed all but lost. Rito had succeeded in his earliest outing against Angel Grove and the Power Rangers.

RITO'S TERRIBLE TRIUMPH

It was no mystery that Rito Revolto, upon first encounter, was a terrifying sight: the bones, the camouflage, the bone sword, etc. He was a frightening figure in his own right, yet he also wielded a secret weapon. During two different battles with the Power Rangers, Rito revealed a hidden transformative ability. In seconds, his right arm could transform into a cannon capable of catastrophic damage. Fortunately, the Power Rangers rarely allowed him to use it.

DESIGNATION

TENGA WARRIORS

Alias (Nickname)
Beak Breath

Known Abilities
Flight,
Super Strength,
The Element
of Suprise

ALPHA 5'S MENACE METER

Run. Please, run.

Take Cover.

▶ Keep Away.

Mostly Harmless.

170

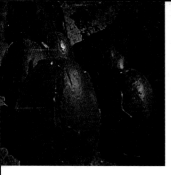

FEATHERED, FREAKISH, AND FEARLESS, THE TENGA WARRIORS WERE BROUGHT TO THE MOON WHILE STILL IN THEIR EGGS BY RITA'S SKELETAL BROTHER, RITO REVOLTO.

The mythical Tenga Warriors were known to be the most ferocious creatures this side of the universe. Outside of their legendary status and supposed rarity, further information regarding the fearsome flying fledglings was nowhere to be found. Even an intense study of Alpha 5's data revealed no further information.

Despite their speech showing some signs of intelligence, the Tengas ultimately weren't much more effective than the Putties that preceded them. Tengas were quick to attack but equally quick to be defeated. With ruffled feathers and fear in their eyes, the bad birds would take to the skies following a failed coup with the Power Rangers. Upon his arrival, Master Vile allegedly supplied the feathered fiends with special seeds to enhance their battle abilities. These seeds worked, causing the Rangers to utilize new and improved Metallic Armor, which was used in further frays against the flying frights. Certainly not the foul force Rita, Zedd, or Vile expected, nevertheless, the Tengas proved to be a continued challenge for the champions of the city.

DESIGNATION
MASTER VILE

Alias (Nickname)
Dad, Father,
Father-in-Law
Known Abilities
TOO MANY
TO COUNT

**ALPHA 5'S
MENACE
METER**

▶ Run. Please, run.

Take Cover.

Keep Away.

Mostly Harmless.

"And now, everyone, party like there's no tomorrow . . . because there's not!"

MUCH OLDER THAN PREVIOUS INVADERS ON EARTH, AND WISER IN THE WAYS OF EVIL, MASTER VILE COMPLETED THE TRIFECTA OF TERRIBLE BEINGS TO TAKE CONTROL OF THE MOON PALACE.

To many, Rita Repulsa was a cruel ruler whose attempts at world domination were often and easily thwarted by the ever-present Power Rangers. Lord Zedd advanced Rita's reign by bringing a fresh perspective to monster creation and Power Ranger manipulation. Master Vile, on the other hand, brought with him a fury and fervor for evil deeds that had not yet been seen by the people of Earth.

Prior to the arrival of Master Vile on the moon, the people of Earth were once again met with a series of furious earthquakes, which rocked the land far and wide. Following the quakes, the sky grew dark—a sign of forthcoming evil. According to Alpha 5's data, Master Vile appeared in Lord Zedd's central throne room and announced his arrival. Zedd, angered and curious as to the identity of this interloper, was given a swift answer to his question. Master Vile, a singular force of evil in the galaxy, was actually Rita's father and, given a recent sharing of marriage vows, Lord Zedd's father-in-law. Humans of all shapes and sizes could understand the immediate effect this must have had on the present Prince of Darkness.

Master Vile had conquered the M-51 galaxy but was hungry for more. After hearing of his daughter and son-in-law's continuous failures, Master Vile set about making some changes. He made it known

173

that he was displeased with Rita's marriage, much to Zedd's frustration. Following that proclamation, Vile unveiled his ultimate plan, which involved the inevitable attainment of the coveted and ancient Zeo Crystal.

The Zeo Crystal was hidden away from Master Vile by the heroic peoples of the M-51 galaxy. Unfortunately, the hiding place happened to be beneath the very Moon Palace in which Master Vile now stood—hidden in the Caves of Deception. The Moon Palace had once been a place of goodness in the galaxy, but was corrupted by Lord Zedd many eons ago. However, the caverns beneath the castle remained untouched by Zedd's evil influence. A force field surrounding the caves prevented anyone who was not pure of heart from touching the Zeo Crystal.

A SUCCESSFUL CAMPAIGN SAW MASTER VILE ARRIVE OVER EARTH IN HIS SKULL CRAFT, KIDNAP THE EVER-RELIABLE NINJOR, AND EVENTUALLY DESTROY THE POWER RANGERS' ZORDS WITH HIS BLUE GLOBBOR MONSTER.

Following his victory, the new Monarch of the Moon decided to throw a party. An End of the World Party. Countless foes of the Power Rangers soon arrived at the Angel Grove Youth Center, where Bulk, Skull, Ernie, and many other citizens stood silently, witnessing a sinister celebration of their downfall. One witness who wished to remain anonymous recalled a moment where the villainous Vile took the stage to command everyone to "party like there's no tomorrow, because there's not!" The monsters

SKULL CRAFT

TERROR IN THE SKY

Seldom seen over Earth, Vile's Skull Craft was a terrifying sight. The ship appeared to be designed to replicate the very skull of its captain. Featuring an open-mouthed, grinning skull and a red gem-like object in the center of its "forehead," Vile's vessel was a pure menace. Fortunately, it was in this same ship that Master Vile fled the moon after his final defeat.

in attendance, of course, burst out into cheers as a burgeoning terror grew within the humans. As the party drew to a close, once again Master Vile took the stage to announce, "Well, everyone, it's been loads of fun but now it's time to activate the Zeo Crystal and destroy the world." This proclamation was followed by skies filled with lightning and a great beam of light from some far-off galaxy, which totaled several buildings in a single blast.

ACCORDING TO ALPHA 5, THE END OF THE WORLD WAS HALTED BY THE POWER RANGERS.

Having traveled to a far-off galaxy (allegedly M-51), the Rangers successfully destroyed the stolen Zeo Crystal, thus stopping Vile's violent agenda. After that series of events, Angel Grove's heroes returned to defeat the Blue Globbor with their recently retrieved Zords and, ultimately, to halt Armageddon. While the Power Rangers succeeded in countering Vile's first assault and all that followed, he still managed to cause much mischief and mayhem during his short time on the moon before his embarrassed and exhausted exit some months later. The Zeo Crystal, now broken and scattered across the cosmos, would return again.

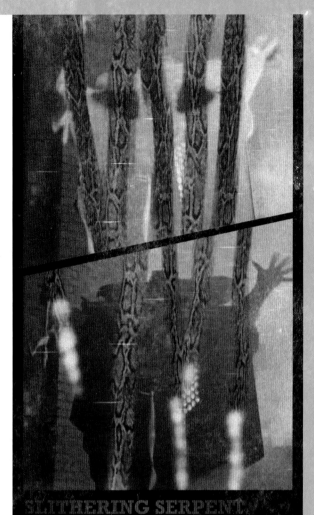

SLITHERING SERPENT
VILE'S SHIFTING SNAKES

Not much is known about the strange serpents that rest within Master Vile's cloak. While Rita Repulsa utilized a magical bicycle on occasion and Lord Zedd preferred Serpentera for transport, Master Vile (Skull Craft aside) utilized a pair of snakes that turned luminescent and transported him from location to location. Apparently, this ability extended to others that might not be in close proximity to the vile villain.

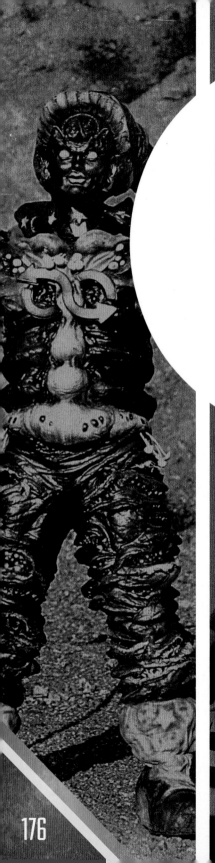

PART TWO

EVIL SPACE ALIENS:
FEAR FROM FAR AND WIDE

DESIGNATION

REPELLATOR

Alias (Nickname)
Green-Pea Soup
Known Abilities
Molecular
Scramblers
(Claws)

SIMILAR IN APPEARANCE TO SILVER HORNS, REPELLATOR WAS A FAR MORE FEROCIOUS

creature. With a disgusting, elongated tongue and a pair of claws, Repellator would have been a challenge for the whole team of Power Rangers. Unfortunately, only the Pink Ranger was present upon the arrival of the ruffian Repellator, due to the other Rangers being off-world on another adventure. Eyewitnesses to the Pink Ranger's battle with Repellator reported that the Pink Ranger seemed to be sick and sneezing. While this began as an inconvenience, eventually Repellator seemed to have contracted the same illness and sneezed uncontrollably. The green aggressor's sneezes began to rock the surrounding landscape with each expulsion. Repellator was transported away soon after, but later reappeared and grew to a colossal size. Fortunately, Repellator was quickly defeated after the arrival of the full team of Power Rangers. During the battle, Repellator's sniffling seemed to have ceased—perhaps he received treatment for his newfound terrestrial illness during his disappearance.

DESIGNATION
VAMPIRUS

Alias (Nickname)
One Ugly Critter
Known Abilities
n/a

VAMPIRUS HATCHED FROM ONE OF THE EGGS GIVEN

to Rita and Zedd as wedding gifts from Rito Revolto. While much was unknown about Vampirus, the few facts regarding the creature were somewhat revealing. Upon receiving the egg, Alpha 5 reported that Zedd and Rita were very excited about the gift. After a series of events that took the Rangers to a far-off location known as the Desert of Despair, Vampirus arrived in that same desert to destroy the temple wherein the Rangers received their powers. If he had succeeded, the Rangers would have been powerless, cut off from the source of the ancient energy that supplied them with their abilities. While Vampirus is greatly feared, he proved to be less than successful in his mission. With the help of Ninjor, the Rangers and their new Ninjazords dispatched the violent villain swiftly and easily.

179

ARTISTMOLE

Alias (Nickname)
Pathetic Picasso
Known Abilities
Laser Brush

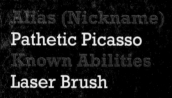

ARTISTMOLE BROUGHT THE RANGERS A NEWFOUND CHALLENGE WITH HIS ABILITY TO

draw both color and the life force out of living beings. According to Alpha 5's information, the Artistmole was created from a dream that first appeared within the subconscious of the Pink Ranger. Zedd and Rita, sensing the Ranger's terrible dream, demanded that Finster use his new device to bring the nightmare to life. The monster-making terrier appeared in the park and zapped the Pink Ranger with his curious creation that brought to life the aggressive Artistmole. In the Rangers' first encounter with the angry artist, Artistmole zapped them with his brush and drained both their color and their powers from them. Along with the Rangers, he also turned an entire neighborhood of the city into shades of gray. Fortunately, with the help of Ninjor, the Rangers were able to wash away the gray and restore the color that Artistmole had removed. Several eyewitnesses reported that during the hand-to-hand combat, the Rangers' strikes seemed to pass right through the Artistmole as if passing through liquid paint. This observation can neither be confirmed nor denied.

DESIGNATION
LANTERRA

YEAR	ORIGIN	TYPE
3		

Alias (Nickname)
Worthless Walking
Lamp Shade
Known Abilities
Flame Breath,
Sword

LANTERRA IS BELIEVED TO HAVE ORIGINATED IN THE SECLUDED JAPANESE GARDEN WITHIN

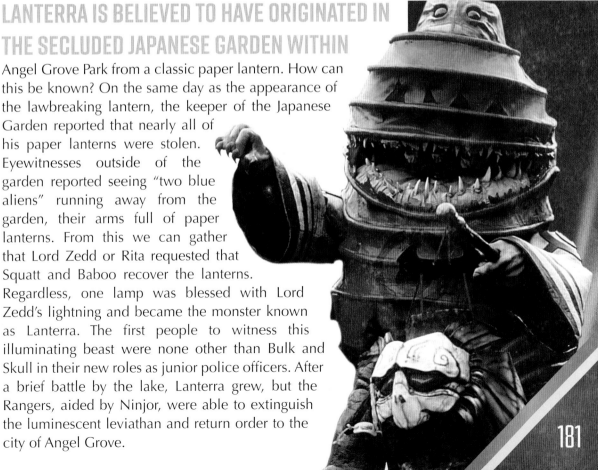

Angel Grove Park from a classic paper lantern. How can this be known? On the same day as the appearance of the lawbreaking lantern, the keeper of the Japanese Garden reported that nearly all of his paper lanterns were stolen. Eyewitnesses outside of the garden reported seeing "two blue aliens" running away from the garden, their arms full of paper lanterns. From this we can gather that Lord Zedd or Rita requested that Squatt and Baboo recover the lanterns. Regardless, one lamp was blessed with Lord Zedd's lightning and became the monster known as Lanterra. The first people to witness this illuminating beast were none other than Bulk and Skull in their new roles as junior police officers. After a brief battle by the lake, Lanterra grew, but the Rangers, aided by Ninjor, were able to extinguish the luminescent leviathan and return order to the city of Angel Grove.

DESIGNATION

MARVO THE MEANIE

Alias (Nickname)
Mr. Walton
Known Abilities
Liquefier Ray,
Chemical Blast

EDUCATORS DESERVE THE UTMOST RESPECT AND ADMIRATION FOR THEIR ABILITY TO

inspire and instruct the young minds of our world—unless they happen to turn into monstrous mischief-making monsters like Marvo the Meanie. The Marvo encounter happened to be the first instance of a resident from Angel Grove being transformed into one of Zedd and Rita's instigative invaders. The victim, Mr. Wilton, was an Angel Grove citizen and a notoriously hard-nosed teacher at the local high school. He was open to revealing his perspective on the event. The Tengas "arrived in the park and began attacking [Wilton] and a student," he disclosed. Shortly after this event, the "skeleton guy showed up and zapped [Wilton] with an odd staff with a Z at the end." This allegedly transformed the unsuspecting educator into "a horrible thing . . . a monster." While Mr. Wilton didn't recall much of the event, he said that at times he remembers certain moments. Ultimately, "[he was] just glad that Angel Grove had the Power Rangers," otherwise he didn't know what would have happened to him. In the end, the Rangers defeated Marvo the Meanie, and Mr. Wilton was returned to his previous form and figure. He soon returned to Angel Grove High, where he still teaches today. According to current staff, he's much nicer to his students.

Alias (Nickname)
Gridiron Geek
Known Abilities
Magic Football with Transformative Powers

CENTIBACK WAS A CREATION UNLIKE ANYTHING FINSTER COULD HAVE IMAGINED ON HIS OWN.

The genesis for the monster involved a lowly centipede and an errant football being tossed about the Moon Palace. The morning that Centiback appeared on Earth at the Angel Grove High football field, the famous quarterback Joe Healy happened to be visiting. The beastly bug utilized its big ball to turn Healy, Bulk, Skull, and several others into living footballs, which fell upon the field. Luckily the Rangers arrived and faced the inconvenient insect on the field. Tengas arrived soon after, and the Power Rangers were forced to face the Centiback and the Tengas as a team in a slapdash game of football. When all of the Rangers except Red were reduced to footballs, the fight moved to the mountains, where the Red Ranger was met by a familiar friend, Ninjor. Together, the Red Ranger and Ninjor retrieved the enchanted football and restored the others to their original form. As snow began to fall in the mountains, Ninjor and the Zords fearlessly faced the insect invader and took him out of the game.

DESIGNATION
HATE MASTER

Alias (Nickname)
Hate *Monster*
Known Abilities
Projectile Hate
Dust

CREATED WITH THE SOLE PURPOSE OF TURNING THE POWER RANGERS AGAINST ONE ANOTHER,

Hate Master nearly succeeded in tearing the team apart. After a brief battle with the Tengas in the park, Zedd and Rita's henchman Squatt was seen collecting dirt from the ground where the fight had just taken place. It was with this dirt (infused with magic by Lord Zedd) that Hate Master turned the team of Rangers into enemies. Upon confronting the new nemesis, all the Rangers except Yellow found themselves sprinkled with a storm of dust that quickly instigated arguments within the team. Eventually, the Rangers came out of their confusion and battled Hate Master with their Zords but were again hit with the strange dust. All seemed lost. Fortunately, the Yellow Ranger was left unaffected and proved her resilience during a one-on-one confrontation with Hate Master by the lake. Somehow, the Yellow Ranger (aided by the always-accessible Alpha 5) reversed the spell once more and defeated Hate Master in the middle of the city.

FACE STEALER

Alias (Nickname)
Blob-O
Known Abilities
Face-Stealing
Beam

THE FACE STEALER WAS ONE OF SEVERAL BEINGS WHOSE ORIGIN RESIDES IN

popular folklore. An exhibit on ancient Kahmalan culture had been erected at the Angel Grove History Museum. Within the extraordinary exhibit were several masks said to have been worn by warriors some five thousand years ago to defeat a ruthless monster known as the Face Stealer. According to legend, the Face Stealer attacked Kahmala for generations on the fourth full moon of each year. This creature would come from the sky and rob the citizens of their faces, leaving them without souls. Fortunately, the Face Stealer was stopped by the masked warriors and captured in an urn for all eternity. Unfortunately, the urn was also on exhibit, leaving it vulnerable to Rita Repulsa's evil spells. After the Face Stealer's release by Rita, the Rangers were initially overcome, and some, indeed, fell victim to the monster's powers. But after utilizing the masks from the museum, the Power Rangers were able to reflect the rampaging monster's face-stealing beam, thus returning all of the stolen faces.

MISS CHIEF

YEAR	ORIGIN	TYPE
3		0

Alias (Nickname)
Cupid

Known Abilities
Love Potion,
Blade Boomerang,
Invisibility

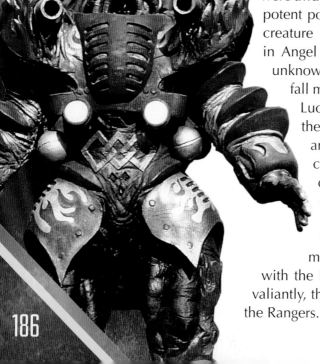

A MONSTROUS MISHANDLING OF THE SAME LOVE POTION USED BY RITA REPULSA ON

Lord Zedd led to some seriously strange circumstances in Angel Grove. According to Alpha 5, while Rita and Zedd were away from the moon, Rito Revolto discovered the potent potion and sprayed it on one of Finster's new creature creations. This love-laced monster arrived in Angel Grove, where it began randomly spraying unknowing citizens, which caused those affected to fall madly in love with whoever was in their sight. Luckily, Miss Chief had already caused unrest on the moon, as witnesses recalled seeing Finster arriving moments later with an antidote that cured all those afflicted. The dazed citizens of Angel Grove were left with a sensation of unknowing—no monster to blame, and no sign of Rita or Zedd. That all changed when Miss Chief suddenly appeared in the mountains and entered into a furious battle with the Power Rangers. Although both sides fought valiantly, the red-hot love monster was extinguished by the Rangers.

DESIGNATION

KATASTROPHE

Alias (Nickname)
Walking Fur Ball
Known Abilities
Shape-Shifting
Sharp Claws

A HUMANOID CAT WITH A BAD ATTITUDE, KATASTROPHE ARRIVED IN ANGEL GROVE AFTER

a series of strange events. Several witness statements confirmed that prior to the beast's arrival, Rita Repulsa was spotted in a suburban area outside the city. One witness claimed that Rita transformed a dumpster into a "pretty nice car," which she then gave to a girl who had been "transformed from a white cat." While this seems odd, it wouldn't be the first time that Rita had been up to mysterious trickery on Earth. The furious feline known as Katastrophe appeared in the suburbs and battled the Power Rangers briefly there before reappearing in the park. There, fully grown, she attempted to scratch her enemies from the ground. With the aid of Ninjor, the Rangers caught the cat by the tail and ended her short encounter in Angel Grove.

DESIGNATION

INCISERATOR

YEAR	ORIGIN	TYPE
3	☾	☆

Alias (Nickname)
Fang Face,
Fangenstein
Known Abilities
Wand

A TRULY GROTESQUE INVADER WITH TWO FACES AND SHARP PROTRUDING FANGS,

Inciserator proved to be a brilliant distraction from Zedd and Rita's true intentions. Inciserator first appeared in Angel Grove Park. Two unsuspecting citizens of the city were terrified when the ghastly grinning ghoul suddenly appeared before them. Understandably, the couple fled the scene on foot. Following the first encounter, Inciserator continued his march of madness through the park, sending bystanders screaming as they ran from the sight of the repellant rascal. The Rangers, absent the Pink Ranger, arrived and battled the fanged freak before he disappeared suddenly, never to be seen again. Unbeknownst to the Power Rangers at the time, Alpha 5 indicated that the fearsome Inciserator was sent as a distraction from the kidnapping of the Pink Ranger at the hands of Goldar.

DESIGNATION

SEE MONSTER

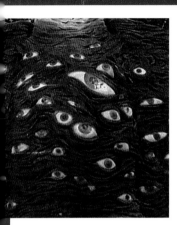

Alias (Nickname)

n/a

Known Abilities

Thought Waves,
Eye Beams

NOT TO BE CONFUSED WITH *SEA* MONSTERS (LIKE COMMANDER CRAYFISH OR PIRANTISHEAD),

See Monster was an eye-covered creature capable of powerful thought waves. A coat-like covering surrounding its body could be pulled back to reveal hundreds upon hundreds of eyes. See Monster emitted a powerful beam that caused terrible pain in the brain. While the extent of these abilities is unknown, his curious magic seemed effective against the Power Rangers for a moment before they were able to push through the spell and return to the battle. Initially appearing in the park, See Monster departed momentarily with the arrival of Rita's ancient Shogunzords. Not much information is available regarding the evil occupation of the Zords. Eventually, the Power Rangers regained control and efficiently ended See Monster.

DESIGNATION
CRABBY CABBIE

YEAR	ORIGIN	TYPE
3		7

Alias (Nickname)
Gas Guzzler
Known Abilities
Exhaust Bomb,
Bigger on the
Inside

ANYONE WHO HAS LIVED IN A BIG CITY OR VISITED ONE WILL KNOW THAT CABS ARE USUALLY

reliable and their drivers very kind. Of course, there are exceptions. However, those exceptions usually don't involve your cab being transformed into a taxi monster with a need for speed. The arrival of the Crabby Cabbie was witnessed by two individuals that need no introduction—Bulk and Skull. After witnessing the theft of a fellow student's car, Bulk, Skull, and the student jumped into a nearby cab, which inexplicably transformed into the fuel-filled freak known as the Crabby Cabbie. Trapped inside the newly minted monster, the three students were fortunate enough to be found by the Power Rangers. Equipped with seemingly new Shark Cycles, the Rangers surrounded the Cabbie and had nearly captured it when Zedd and Rita cast down their spell to make the monster grow. During the ensuing battle between the Crabby Cabbie and the Shogunzords, the three passengers were saved by Alpha 5 via the villainous vehicle's exhaust pipe. After driving through and destroying a nearby building, the Rangers were able to wreck the crazed car, thus saving Angel Grove from another dangerous driver.

DESIGNATION

GARBAGE MOUTH

Alias (Nickname)
n/a
Known Abilities
Energy Beam
Trash Bin

THE APPEARANCE OF GARBAGE MOUTH CERTAINLY SENT SHOCKWAVES

through Angel Grove. A lizard-like creature with a tail and webbed fingers, it sported a trash-can-lid hat which gave it its strange moniker. The foul-smelling fiend first arrived just outside the Angel Grove Hospital. Eyewitnesses reported that the terrible being transformed from an everyday trash can into a blue-green gruesome gargoyle. The Power Rangers were quickly on the scene. Bulk and Skull, along with local police official Lieutenant Stone, exited the hospital and briefly witnessed the battle between the trash-bin buffoon and the Rangers before "requesting reinforcements." During the battle, one unknown young blond woman fell into the hands of the trashy terror before evidently freeing herself and fleeing. After the monster suddenly grew to a large size, the Power Rangers summoned their Shogunzords. Garbage Mouth was ultimately "thrown to the curb" and the hospital remained safe.

RAVENATOR

Alias (Nickname)

Gastric Geek

Known Abilities

**Insatiable
Appetite**

RAVENATOR WAS BLESSED WITH AN INSATIABLE APPETITE AND MOLARS

to match. A gruesome invader who threatened to "eat all of Angel Grove," Ravenator was always prepared to indulge in his fearsome feasting habits wearing his trademark apron. According to Alpha 5's data, when this hungry horror first appeared in Angel Grove, he was a shrunken, pint-size pest who snuck into the White Ranger's food. When the White Ranger ate this tainted food, Ravenator took up a temporary home in the Ranger's stomach, which caused some ill effects. Alpha 5 reported that, suddenly burdened with an uncontrollable appetite, the White Ranger would not stop feasting. After discovering the problem, the Rangers were able to force the feasting fiend to leave the stomach of their friend and grow to his regular size. This confrontation, the first and last, took place in the park near the picnic tables. Even though the monster had grown to enormous proportions, the Rangers cancelled the Ravenator's reservation and destroyed him with a swift swipe of the Shogunzord Saber.

BRICK BULLY

Alias (Nickname)
Blockhead
Known Abilities
Rock Bombs,
Brick Beams

THE BRICK BULLY, AWAKENED BY A BOLT OF MAGIC FROM RITA'S STAFF, QUICKLY EXITED

the newly cleaned brick wall that had been its home. The clay creature (no relation to the Putties) immediately proceeded to harass the Humanitarian Housing Project area of which the wall had been a part. Although the Rangers were the only individuals present at the time, several witnesses saw from a distance a beam of energy hit the bordering brick wall and transform into the Brick Bully before their eyes. Apparently, the Rangers were there to deal with Squatt, Baboo, and Rito, who had arrived earlier and had begun roughing up the newly renovated space. As soon as the Brick Bully entered the scene, it expelled its brick beam, instantly transforming all of the Rangers (except for the Pink and Blue Rangers) into actual bricks! According to Alpha 5's data, the Rangers weren't *actually* turned into bricks but were, instead, miniaturized and encased in the clay confines. Soon after those events, the Brick Bully grew and stood towering over the Angel Grove suburbs, where it was met by the Blue Ranger's Shogunzord. After a brief battle, which saw the Zord unaffected by being encased in brick, the Blue Ranger succeeded in bringing down the walking wall once and for all.

DESIGNATION
SINISTER SIMIAN

Alias (Nickname)
Kelly
Known Abilities
Power Punch,
Power Blast,
Teleportation

EARLIER IN THE DAY, ERNIE, OF ANGEL GROVE'S YOUTH CENTER, CALLED LOCAL POLICE TO

report that a large shipment of bananas had gone missing from his stock. Bulk and Skull, then junior police officers, set about trying to find the culprit. Their quest brought them to the suburbs, where they stumbled upon an escaped simian whose name, they learned, was Kelly. Having been brought to Angel Grove by a well-known Australian educator, Kelly was meant to be a part of a guest lecture at Angel Grove University later that day. How she ended up in the suburbs remains unknown. Bulk and Skull proceeded to take the newfound chimp to the park, where she reportedly became attracted to a local fruit stand. There, with some help from Zedd's lightning, the cheerful chimp was changed into the chest-beating beast known to Angel Grove as the Sinister Simian! Teleported to a nearby jungle gym, the Sinister Simian sent parents into a frenzy as they quickly gathered up their children and evacuated the park. The Power Rangers arrived soon after to distract the Sinister Simian and douse her with a dose of an antidote, which brought the mammoth monkey back to her normal state. It should be noted that Ernie's missing bananas had not been stolen, but rather simply misplaced. No monkey business there.

BLUE GLOBBOR

Alias (Nickname)
n/a
Known Abilities
Sword,
Power Drain,
Morphin Ability

MUCH HAS BEEN SAID PREVIOUSLY ABOUT THE

arrival of the Rangers' ultimate foe, Master Vile, and his sudden appearance in Angel Grove. It is equally as important to focus on the Blue Globbor, Vile's first violent villain. According to Alpha 5's files, the Blue Globbor was hatched from an egg extracted from Master Vile's mouth with the intent of capturing and destroying the Power Rangers' ally Ninjor. First appearing in the park, the Globbor was met by a massive Ninjor, who attempted to fend off the furious freak to no avail. The Globbor disappeared with Ninjor in tow and later reappeared to attack the city. When the Power Rangers arrived, our hometown heroes soon discovered that the gargantuan Globbor had the ability to sap their power. As the Rangers fought a challenging battle, Vile made Globbor grow in size. When he did, he replicated armor similar to that of Ninjor upon his body. The cunning Vile had managed to connect Globbor and Ninjor—any attack against Globbor would harm Ninjor as well. After the Power Rangers' Zords were seemingly destroyed, the unstoppable team came back from the brink of destruction and finally blighted the Blue Globbor. And as Master Vile retreated, he made a resounding remark: *"Monsters come and go, but I won't be so easily destroyed, Rangers!"*

DESIGNATION

DISCHORDIA

Alias (Nickname)
n/a
Known Abilities
Villainous Voice,
Sword

DISCHORDIA WAS MASTER VILE'S SECOND CREATION AND WAS FAR LESS OF A SUCCESS

than the previous monsters. This singing scoundrel first appeared in the suburbs outside the city, where she was met by the Power Rangers. Within an instant, the villain Dischordia had the Rangers dancing to and fro across the pavement, unable to stop. Dischordia's "gift," a villainous voice with mind-control capabilities, enchanted the protectors of the city and nearly defeated them. At one point, a bystander witnessed the White Ranger resisting the urge to present his Power Coin to the musical monstrosity. Somehow the Rangers morphed into their protective Metallic Armor, thus blocking out Dischordia's hypnotic spell. As Dischordia suddenly grew large, she raised her saber to the sky and was met by darkening clouds and a violent storm of lightning that seemed to embrace her. Alpha 5's data indicated that this sudden storm recharged the rampaging rival of the Rangers, preparing her for the ensuing battle. Fortunately, Ninjor glided in on his cloud and launched a joint attack with the Shogunzords and Titanus. The three forces combined their powers and silenced Dischordia's damaging declarations.

196

THE END TIMES
RANGERS IN REVERSE

THE TURNING OF TIME

THE FALL OF THE MIGHTY MORPHIN POWER RANGERS AND THE DAY THE EARTH TURNED BACKWARD

THIS CHILLING AND UNTHINKABLE EVENT MAY SEEM UNFAMILIAR TO EVEN THE MOST KNOWLEDGEABLE ANGEL GROVE HISTORIAN. ALPHA 5'S FILES SHOCKINGLY REVEAL A SAGA THAT REMAINED LOST UNTIL NOW.

On February 4, 1995, Lord Zedd briefly utilized the ancient Rock of Time to reverse Earth's spin and revert the citizens of our planet to their earlier ages. While this was indeed a terrifying experience, the events of that day were largely forgotten by those affected by the Rock and its powers. Angel Grove's protectors had succeeded in halting Lord Zedd and Rita Repulsa once more.

For three years, the Mighty Morphin Power Rangers, Zordon, and Alpha 5 had been successful in keeping our planet and the citizens of Angel Grove safe from otherworldly threats. A poisonous pollinator, a sinister sphinx, a guitar-wielding cicada, and even a rapping pumpkin patch were continually thwarted in their vicious attacks on the city. Even when the Rangers fell or seemed doomed, they always managed to defeat the enemy. They were the heroes of Angel Grove. They were the heroes of Earth. And on November 27, 1995, our Power Rangers fell

in the face of Master Vile's most violent and unexpected assault.

That morning, like any other in Angel Grove, citizens went about their business, aware of a potential encounter, something that had become second nature for those who decided to stay in the quaint, coastal town. When reports came in of a sudden and unexplainable quake on the moon, a collective shiver ran up the spines of those below. Apparently, Vile had summoned a special sphere from the darkness within the moon. Inside of this sphere remained a power capable of destroying our planet and all of its inhabitants—the Orb of Doom. Master Vile sent Rito Revolto to Earth to place the Orb of Doom in a specific location to the north of Angel Grove. A treacherous crystal, it had the ability to stop Earth's rotation and reverse time when placed at the proper longitude and latitude.

The Power Rangers arrived in the mountains moments after Rito's arrival, aware of the immediate danger posed by the Orb of Doom. Rito was expecting them and released a horde of the horrendous Tenga Warriors to distract and hold back the team. To further divide and distract the Power Rangers, Rito ordered half of the Tengas to descend upon the civilian carnival at the base of the mountain. The super team divided their ranks, and half of them sped off to stop the stampede of Tengas advancing toward the carnival. There they met Goldar, further delaying their return to the mountain. Overwhelmed and outnumbered, the remaining Rangers did their best to beat back the Tengas and reach Rito. Unfortunately, the crazed crows proved too powerful. In a triumphant moment, Rito Revolto placed the Orb directly into the ground.

INSTANTLY, A BLINDING BEAM OF LIGHT ERUPTED FROM THE MOUNTAINS, AND THE EARTH SHOOK AS THE ORB'S POWER TOOK HOLD ON OUR PEACEFUL PLANET.

Having succeeded in their plans, Rito and Goldar departed back to the moon with their troupe of Tenga Warriors. They would surely be rewarded for their success.

For a few brief minutes, the citizens of Angel Grove stood in awe, looking toward the sky—and the moon. They witnessed another beam, this time tearing from the moon and into the sky above their heads. Lightning soon filled the sky, and the mountains seemed to roar in pain as the natural progression of planet Earth was halted. Suddenly, and without any sign, Earth began to rotate in the wrong direction. Memories of marriages and long-held love vanished from the minds of innocent earthlings who were turned back into unknowing infants and youngsters. Those who were too young simply disappeared altogether, along with any memory of them ever having existed. These were dark times, indeed.

From over the mountains strode the colossal forms of Rita Repulsa, Lord Zedd, Goldar, and Rito Revolto, to claim what was then rightfully theirs. They had defeated the Power Rangers, who were nowhere to be seen. No Zords were called and, therefore, none arrived. And so, those four fearsome aliens from far, far away marched confidently across the carnival, laughing in the face of those they had conquered. While they enjoyed their success for as long as they were able, the monsters from the moon would soon learn that Earth is protected. Not just by the Mighty Morphin Power Rangers. Not just by Zordon and Alpha 5. But also by beings similar to themselves. Soon they would meet the Mighty Morphin Alien Rangers.

YEAR FOUR

(1996)

A WELCOMING TO OUR WORLD

PART ONE

AQUITIAN AVENGERS

THEY CAME IN PEACE

THE MIGHTY MORPHIN ALIEN RANGERS

After the arrival
and occupation of Earth's moon by the
extraterrestrial entities known as Lord Zedd
and Rita Repulsa, it was easy to forget that not all
visitors from other worlds are evil. After three years
of evil invasions, it was understandable that the arrival
of a new alien force would potentially be met with
fear. It is a sad fact that almost all the citizens of Angel
Grove and around the world will never truly know the
significance of our celestial saviors.
Fortunately, through Alpha 5's rigorous documentation
of the events, we understand a bit more about how
five fascinating and friendly extraterrestrials
from the planet Aquitar came to our planet
and protected it from evil.

A WORLD UNACCUSTOMED

THE EFFECT OF TIME TRAVEL ON THE CITIZENS OF ANGEL GROVE

PRIOR TO MASTER VILE TURNING BACK TIME, THE PEOPLE OF ANGEL GROVE HAD GROWN ACCUSTOMED TO THE PLETHORA OF PERTURBING MONSTERS MARCHING THROUGH THEIR CITY. WHILE THEY HAD REMAINED AWARE, THEY KNEW THAT THE POWER RANGERS WOULD SOON ARRIVE AND SAVE THE DAY.

Not only did turning back time reduce adults to teens, and teens to children, and children to nothing, it also placed the citizens of Angel Grove in a time before the Power Rangers. Not only were there no Power Rangers, but there had never been a Rita Repulsa, either. There had never been the grumbling, gravelly voice of Lord Zedd booming through the thunderous skies.

There had never been the gold-plated ape and the camouflaged bag of bones up to unknown mischief. At this point in time (presumably around ten years before Rita would escape her space dumpster), the days came and went as per usual: no monsters, no beams of light from the moon, and no multicolored superheroes in alien armor.

When the citizens looked to the sky to see Lord Zedd, Rita Repulsa, Goldar, and Rito Revolto towering over their city, they panicked. They'd never seen extraordinary extraterrestrials before. After several terrifying minutes of reckless destruction, the monsters abruptly vanished. The city of Angel Grove went into lockdown. A mandatory curfew was put in place to protect citizens from unexpected attacks.

The aliens had arrived; the new faces of evil

AND THEN THERE CAME FIVE . . .

THE ARRIVAL OF FIVE
THE ALIEN RANGERS OF AQUITAR

WHILE THE WORLD HAD FORGOTTEN ABOUT THEIR HEROES, TWO VERY IMPORTANT INDIVIDUALS HAD NOT. ALPHA 5 AND ZORDON HAD BEEN UNAFFECTED BY EARTH'S REVERSAL, AND THEY SET OUT TO FIND A GROUP OF POWERFUL NEW PROTECTORS.

THE WATER-WORLD OF AQUITAR

The planet Aquitar is 100 percent covered in water. Life on Aquitar exists solely beneath the waves, where the citizens of the planet, called Aquitians, live in pod-like structures. While this culture exists beneath the water, they are remarkably humanoid and share many common traits with those of human beings. Almost all forms of life on Earth require oxygen for survival, and all forms of life on Aquitar require energy derived from the clean water of their planet. Initially, Zordon was concerned about asking the Aquitian Rangers to intervene on Earth. However, the need for immediate assistance overwhelmed him with worry and he requested that Alpha 5 send out a distress call to Aquitar at once.

A Galactic Alert Transmission was sent from the Command Center via a large beam that erupted from the top of the structure. The beam, green in color, reached Aquitar in minutes. There, the Alien Rangers received the call and immediately contacted Zordon. Hearing of Master Vile's treachery and hold over the planet, the Aquitians agreed to travel across the stars to assist in ridding Earth of its "most unwelcome visitor." With them, the Alien Rangers brought their own Zord-like engines of power—the Battle Borgs. Given to them over a century ago by the one and only Ninjor, the Battle Borgs were able to be controlled telepathically by the Aquitian Rangers. And so, the Mighty Morphin Alien Rangers arrived on Earth with one goal: to destroy evil and protect all that is good. We, the people of Earth, owe them our lives.

PART TWO

EVIL SPACE ALIENS:
AN UNEXPECTED EVIL

A GROTESQUE GATHERING

MASTER VILE'S MONSTER CONFERENCE

THERE'S NO BIGGER FAN OF GATHERING TOGETHER A PLETHORA OF DISGUSTING DEVIANTS THAN MASTER VILE.

Similar to his End of the World Party thrown in celebration of his looming victory over the Power Rangers, Vile's Monster Conference featured a guest list of frighteningly fearsome freaks from all four corners of the universe. This monumental meeting within the Moon Palace was called in order to respond to the sudden and unexpected arrival of the Alien Rangers. The crudely crowded gathering brought together the likes of the Crabby Cabbie, Brick Bully, Miss Chief, See Monster, Lanterra, Arachnofiend, Smudgey Swirl, Yetiki, Piecemeal, Parrot Top, and Barkzo, along with Professor Longnose.

The Moon Palace and the moon had been rocked by the arrival of the force of good known as the Aquitian Rangers. Master Vile was out for revenge. No one would interfere with his success, least of all other invaders from another planet. Out of the macabre meeting of monstrous beings, Master Vile chose a select few to travel to Earth and confront the new Mighty Morphin Alien Rangers. This team, led by Professor Longnose, who apparently took a break from conquering a faraway Dark Galaxy

star, arrived in the craggy, desert mountainscape outside Angel Grove.

When the platoon of goons arrived, the police of Angel Grove sounded the alarm signifying an immediate enactment of the curfew. They would soon be under attack, and without any means of battling the beastly bad guys, all they could do was wait. Moments later, the Aquitian Rangers made their debut by transporting to the mountains, fully morphed, and faced off against their newfound foes. After an initial encounter that saw the Rangers battle the Crabby Cabbie, See Monster, Garbage Mouth, and many others, Master Vile made his play and cast down his power, which encircled the gang of grisly creatures and grew them to their secondary size. Towering above the mountains and now visible to the citizens of Angel Grove, Professor Longnose led his team against the Aquitians. But soon after, the Alien Rangers called upon their Battle Borgs and the real battle finally began. After a testing trial of Borg versus beast, the Mighty Morphin Alien Rangers, Angel Grove's new protectors, were joined by the Shogun Megazord, and with their combined powers, they slew the pestering Professor Longnose. Fearful of a similar fate, the remaining ranks cut their losses and transported out and away from the battlefield.

VILE VANQUISHED

THE ABRUPT VANISHING OF MASTER VILE

AS THE BARRAGE OF BEASTIES FLED FOR THEIR LIVES BACK TO WHO KNOWS WHERE, TENSIONS AT THE MOON PALACE ROSE SIGNIFICANTLY.

As with Zedd and Rita before him, Master Vile had not been able to wholly succeed in his attempted takeover of planet Earth. While the citizens of Angel Grove applauded the arrival of the Aquitian Rangers and their swift defeat of Professor Longnose and his legion of loathsome leviathans, Master Vile had to face the fact that perhaps Earth was far too high of a hurdle to clear. And with this revelation, according to Alpha 5's often accurate data, Master Vile threw a fit and abruptly left the Moon Palace, returning to his home planet. Perhaps there, wherever there is, Master Vile will find the success he was hoping for on Earth; we can only hope he doesn't. While Vile had evacuated the moon, there remained the constant threat that had been there since day one—Rita Repulsa, and her horror of a husband, Lord Zedd. To say that Alpha 5 and Zordon felt relief at Vile's departure would be wishful thinking. The threat still existed and the invasive forces from the Moon Palace would surely continue, but at least the Rangers would be facing familiar foes. And so, the saga of the Aquitian Rangers began with a boom and would make for an extremely exciting affair that would last only a short while.

DESIGNATION
SLOTSKY

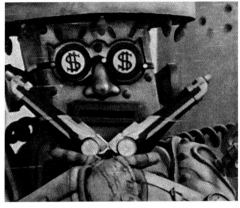

Alias (Nickname)
Regenerator
Known Abilities
Super Magnet

THE DAY LEADING UP TO SLOTSKY'S ENCOUNTER WITH

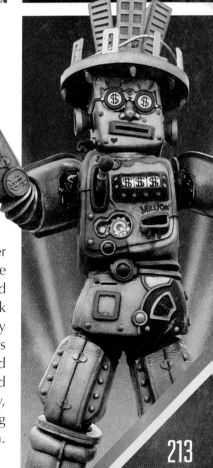

the Alien Rangers was filled with frightful and horrible hurdles. Zedd, out from under the thumb of Rita's father, set to work on a plan to rid the Power Rangers of their Power Coins. The Blue Ranger worked tirelessly with the Aquitians to develop a Regenerator that would allow him and his teammates to return to their natural age and resume their duties as Power Rangers. But after interference from Rito and Goldar, the Blue Ranger only succeeded in re-aging himself before both the Regenerator and the Power Coins were taken from him. Rita and Zedd quickly destroyed the Power Coins and transformed the Regenerator into the steel-clad Slotsky. The Aquitians, who had retreated to the Angel Grove Park fountain for rehydration, were soon met by Slotsky and an army of Tengas. After a momentary tussle that saw the Alien Rangers lose their blasters to Slotsky's super magnet, the Aquitians rallied behind their Borgs. Slotsky, now grown by Rita and Zedd, arrived near the quarry with his powers quickly increasing. Fortunately, our fearless friends from outer space succeeded in destroying the mechanical monster only minutes after the battle had begun.

BARBARIC BROTHERS

YEAR	ORIGIN	TYPE
4		?

Alias (Nickname)
Erik and Merrick
Known Abilities
Erik: Saw
Merrick: Drill
Poison Pollutant

AFTER ARRIVING ON EARTH, THE AQUITIANS WORKED WITH THE BLUE RANGER AND ALPHA 5

to develop a clean water supply similar to that of Aquitar. On this day, the Blue Ranger had successfully developed a molecular hydro-atmospheric generator that would purify the waters of Angel Grove Lake for the Aquitian Rangers. Catching wind of the plan, Lord Zedd sent Goldar and Rito to retrieve the device. When their attempts were thwarted, the Master of the Moon sent two new monsters, Erik and Merrick Barbaric.

The Barbaric Brothers arrived with a potent pollutant. They poured this toxin into the lake, causing the water to turn purple and be rendered contaminated. Zedd decided to sic the sinister siblings on the rest of the world, too, starting with Angel Grove. Luckily, they didn't make it past the park. Soon after the towering twosome arrived, so did the Aquitian Rangers' Battle Borgs. Even with their newly advanced armor and weaponry, the Barbaric Brothers stood no chance against the combined force of the Borgs and the arrival of the Shogun Megazord. One more battle won, the Rangers returned to find that Goldar and Rito had succeeded in destroying the hydro-atmospheric generator. The Aquitians would have to return home.

Alias (Nickname)
Dough Head
Known Abilities
Wrist Blasters, Thunder Stomp

THE FOLLOWING ENCOUNTER IS A TEXTBOOK EXAMPLE OF RITA AND ZEDD'S UNENDING

villainy and hatred for the human race. While many young folks of Angel Grove were enjoying a sunny day at Splash City, a water park, the crazy couple on the moon kept watch. The Aquitians had successfully returned to Aquitar and rehydrated, feeling much better in their own waters. Sensing this moment of weakness, Rita and Zedd crossed staffs and created a new monster that emerged midway through the day at the water park. Alpha 5 reported that this was no mere monster created from an object; this monster was created from a child at the park—a bully. The data did not reveal a name nor did it include a description of the child, though perhaps that is for the best. Fortunately, the Alien Rangers were able to make a return trip within moments. After a series of small fights, the Aquitians were able to talk down the boisterous Brat Boy, causing him to revert to the young boy within. Upon waking up from the transformative state that he'd been placed in, the boy allegedly believed that the whole experience had been a dream.

WITCHBLADE

Alias (Nickname)
An Old Friend
(Zedd's)
Known Abilities
Blades, Swords
(a lot of sharp
things)

HAVING RETURNED TO EARTH ONCE AGAIN, THE AQUITIANS SET OUT ON THEIR QUEST TO FIND

clean, fresh water for their rehydration process. The friendly aliens visited the local marine aquarium of Angel Grove (at the request of the Blue Ranger) where they conferred with some of the underwater wildlife as to the locations of nearby sources of clean water. During their visit, the Alien Rangers discovered that a river running through the forest outside Angel Grove might hold the hydration source they required. Cestro, the Blue Alien Ranger, soon teleported to the quarry located near the river. There he was confronted by an old friend of Lord Zedd—Witchblade. Already weakened by dehydration, Cestro struggled to battle the beast beneath the burning sunlight. Soon after, the battle moved to the forest, where the remaining Alien Rangers arrived. Once grown, Witchblade nearly overpowered the Aquitians. Ever resourceful, the Alien Rangers called upon the Shogunzords and quickly melted the hateful hag.

ARACHNOFIEND

YEAR	ORIGIN	TYPE
4		

Alias (Nickname)
Itsy-Bitsy Spider
Known Abilities
Web of Deceit,
Energy Blast

DETERMINED TO FIND A WAY FOR THE ORIGINAL POWER RANGERS TO REGAIN THEIR POWERS,

Zordon and the Blue Ranger agreed that finding and joining scattered Zeo Crystal pieces might just do the trick. Zedd and Rita, on the other hand, were determined to stop them no matter what. As the Blue Ranger returned to his lab with the final piece of tech required to reassemble the Crystal, he suddenly found himself attacked and abducted by a webbed weirdo known as Arachnofiend. Alerted by Alpha 5 and Zordon, the Alien Rangers tracked the Blue Ranger to a chilling cave coated with layers of silky spiderwebs. There, among Arachnofiend's other prey, the Aquitians discovered the web-bound Blue Ranger. A clever trap had been set and the Alien Rangers were now within Arachnofiend's web of deceit. Eventually, after freeing their tied-up teammate, the Aquitians escaped with the Blue Ranger to find Arachnofiend towering over them via one of Lord Zedd's growth bombs. Over the industrial park at the edge of the city, the Alien Rangers battled the beastly bipedal spider fiend and brought it to its knees with the flaming blade of the Shogun Megazord.

217

HYDRO HOG

Alias (Nickname)
Wart Breath

Known Abilities
Water Drain,
Hydration Sap,
Fire Breath

HAVING REDUCED OTHER PLANETS TO DRY WASTELANDS, THE HYDRO HOG SET HIS SIGHTS

on a new target thanks to Lord Zedd and Rita Repulsa. According to the Aquitian Rangers, the big-boned beast with beady black eyes known as Hydro Hog was their equivalent to Lord Zedd. Finster attempted to bring this repugnant ruler, often referred to as the Emperor of Dark Waters, to Earth before Zordon blocked his efforts. However, Lord Zedd later set a trap for Zordon, tricking the kind leader into blocking a second attempt at bringing the Hydro Hog to Earth. In reality, Zedd had already sent the beast to Angel Grove's lake.

Citizens enjoying the lapping waves were met with the frightful face of an alien being. Immediately, the Alien Rangers arrived on the beach to face their long-fought foe, but they were met with little success. After stealing two of the Rangers' swords and defeating them in a duel, Hydro Hog created a vortex that successfully sucked up all the water in the lake. The Emperor of Dark Waters then proceeded to drain the life force from the nearly defeated Aquitians by placing his hand on their shoulders. All seemed lost when Alpha 5 transported the Alien Rangers to the local pool, hoping for

hydration but finding an empty hole. The Hydro Hog had moved quickly in draining water sources worldwide.

Clouds created by Hydro Hog covered Earth. Quickly, the Blue Ranger of the original Mighty Morphin Power Rangers developed a device that would cause the clouds to give up their hold on the world's water supply. Turning on the device brought forth a rainfall that covered Angel Grove for only a few minutes. But it was enough. The Alien Rangers, now rehydrated and rejuvenated, kicked into gear and confronted their archenemy in the center of the city. Suddenly grown by the magic of Rita and Zedd, Hydro Hog successfully caught the Shogun Megazord's fiery sword inches away from his face. No monster had ever achieved such a feat. Fortunately, the arrival of the mythic Falconzord halted the water-stealing savage. Moments after the fall of the Hydro Hog, Earth's waters were returned and a sense of peace once again flowed through the air of Angel Grove.

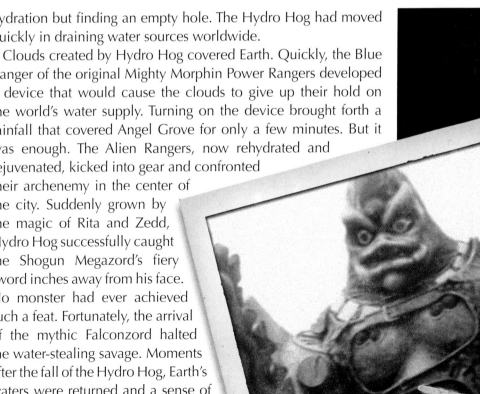

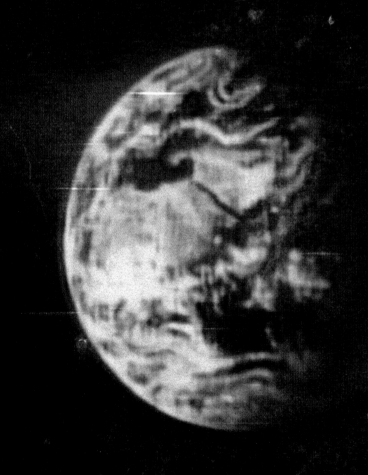

WHEN TIME WAS FINALLY RETURNED TO ITS NATURAL FLOW, IT BROUGHT A SENSE OF ACCOMPLISHMENT AND PEACE TO THE CITIZENS OF ANGEL GROVE.

The Hydro Hog had been destroyed. Master Vile had fled the galaxy, running back to his own planet like a petulant child. The world rejoiced as its waters returned, thanks to the welcomed guests from Aquitar. With time in its proper order, the citizens of Angel Grove waited with bated breath for their favorite Rangers to return—the Mighty Morphin Power Rangers. However, something completely unexpected and devastating was about to take place. While the Alien Rangers worked tirelessly to restore Earth's waters, Rita and Zedd had hatched an unseen and unknowable plan. Goldar and Rito had secretly managed to find their way beneath the Command Center. There, in complete secrecy, they planted a device capable of reducing the Power Rangers' home base to a pile of rubble.

Moments before the device was triggered, the Power Rangers escaped the Command Center thanks to Alpha 5 and Zordon's sacrifice. Standing among the mountains, the Power Rangers witnessed their beloved Command Center reduced to dust. Amid the rubble, they located the Zeo Crystal, which they believed had been stolen by Rito and Goldar moments before the blast. While Goldar and Rito had succeeded in escaping, they had dropped the Crystal in the blast, losing all memory of their lives before that moment. On the moon, Rita Repulsa and Lord Zedd packed up their lives as quickly as possible into Serpentera as a new force of evil moved ever closer to our Earth. The Machine Empire, conquerers of countless galaxies, had caught Earth in their sights. Even Rita and Zedd were hesitant.

The Power Rangers were left without powers. Goldar and Rito were abandoned on Earth without a clue as to their identities. The Machine Empire suddenly hovered overhead, far more fearsome and furious than any force that had attempted an attack on Earth before. All seemed uncertain. However, Angel Grove has seen unspeakable acts of evil. And through it all, the citizens have triumphed.

The universe is full of mysteries beyond our understanding. Our own galaxy has hardly been explored by those who call it home. While aliens may try to annihilate humankind, the Power Rangers have always and will always continue to block their attempts. While I have not met a Power Ranger or even managed a meeting with Alpha 5 beyond our initial contact, I know they're out there every day making sure that we're safe. The Power Rangers have protected us. In return, it is important that we remember their most menacing foes and the courage it took to overcome them in the face of unimaginable odds.

INDEX

Gabriel P. Cooper is an amateur UFOlogist, cryptozoologist, and an avid comic book reader. He grew up in Michigan and now spends his time between Angel Grove and Brooklyn, New York. This is his first work of nonfiction.

SPECIAL THANKS TO

the Angel Grove Historical Society, the Angel Grove Public Library and Archives, the *Angel Grove Gazette*, Channel 6 News, Eugene "Skull" Skullovitch, Farkas "Bulk" Bulkmeier, my editors, Max Bisantz and Rob Valois, at Penguin Random House, and Saban Brands.